"What has happened to you, Celia?" he said roughly.

"What do you mean?" she gasped. She went very still and stared at the hard angle of his jaw above the high collar of his doublet. A muscle flexed there and his lips were pressed in an angry line.

"You look like the Celia I remember," he said. One hand slid slowly down her arm, rubbing her velvet sleeve over her skin until he touched her bare wrist. Something flared in his eyes as he felt the leap of her pulse, and he twined his fingers with hers.

Celia was too frozen to pull away. She felt like the hawk's prey, in truth—mesmerized as he swooped closer and closer.

"You're even more beautiful than you were then," he said, his voice softer and deeper. "But your eyes are hard."

Celia jerked in his arms. "You mean I am not the foolish, gullible girl who can be lured by a man's pretty words? I have learned my lesson well since we last met, John, and I'm grateful for it."

* * *

Tarnished Rose of the Court
Harlequin® Historical #1110—October 2012

D0596161

Tarnished Rose of the Court

AMANDA McCABE

HARLEQUIN®

entertain, enrich, inspire™

Recycling programs for this product may not exist in your area.

ISBN-13: 978-0-373-29710-8

TARNISHED ROSE OF THE COURT

Copyright © 2012 by Ammanda McCabe

This edition published by arrangement with Harlequin Books S.A.

For questions and comments about the quality of this book, please contact us at CustomerService@Harlequin.com.

® and TM are trademarks of Harlequin Enterprises Limited or its corporate affiliates. Trademarks indicated with ® are registered in the United States Patent and Trademark Office, the Canadian Trade Marks Office and in other countries.

www.Harlequin.com

Printed in U.S.A.

**Did you know that these novels are also
available as ebooks? Visit www.Harlequin.com.**

To the Martini Club—
Alicia Dean, Christy Gronlund, Kathy Wheeler!

Thanks for the inspiration,
and for always keeping Friday nights fun…

Chapter One

Whitehall Palace, December 1564

It *was* him.

Suddenly dizzy, Celia Sutton reached out to steady herself against the panelled wall of Queen Elizabeth's presence chamber. The thick crowd had pressed in around her again, obscuring her view with a sea of jewelled velvet and embroidered satin. The nervous laughter and high-pitched chatter as they waited anxiously to petition the Queen sounded like a flock of birds in her ears, buzzing and formless.

She rubbed her hand over her eyes and looked again, standing on tiptoe to try and peer over the crowd. She could no longer see him. Not even that tiny glimpse of his tall figure by the door. The flash of his careless grin. He was gone.

Or maybe he had never been there at all. Maybe it had just been her imagination playing tricks on her. She had not been sleeping well—had spent too many late nights here at Queen Elizabeth's Christmas revels. She had too many worries, and it was wearing on her. That was all.

And yet—he had looked so *real*.

"It was not him," she whispered. John Brandon was gone. She had not seen him for over three years—three very long, hard years—and she would never see him again. What was more, she did not *want* to see him. It would only remind her of the foolish girl she'd once been, of her old weakness for his handsome face, and right now she needed all her strength.

She pushed herself away from the wall and took a deep breath, trying to stand perfectly still, to keep herself calm. The Queen would call for her soon, and she had to have all her wits about her when they met. Her entire life depended on it. She should look only to the future now, not to the past. Not to John Brandon.

But still that fleeting image lingered in her mind, that glimpse of his lean, muscled figure through the crowd and the pounding of her heart at the sight. Despite the roaring fire in the stone grates, the close press of the crowd, and her own fur-trimmed black and purple velvet gown, she shivered.

All around her were desperate faces—people who saw their last chance in catching the Queen's attention. Did she look like them? She feared it was so. What would John say if he could see her now? Would he even recognise her?

The door to the Queen's privy chamber opened and everyone's attention turned towards it in the hope their name would now be called. Hope sank down again when they saw it was only Anton Gustavson and Lord Langley, the last parties to be called to consult with Queen Elizabeth. The nervous chatter fluttered anew.

Celia froze when her gaze met Anton's. He was her long-lost Swedish cousin, recently arrived in England to lay his claim to their grandfather's estate at Briony Manor. That estate was Celia's last hope for a comfortable, independent life in which she did not have to answer to the whims of a cruel man any longer. But as she had watched Anton charm the Queen, and every other lady at Court, her hopes had slipped away. He would have the estate, and she would be thrown back to the dubious mercy of her late husband's family.

Anton gave her a wary nod, and she curtsied in answer. He was the only family she had left, yet she did not know him and could not trust him. That was one of the hard lessons John Brandon had once taught her— never to trust in appearances or emotions. Always to be cautious.

Anton's latest flirtation, the beautiful golden-blonde Rosamund Ramsay, came to his side and gently touched his arm. He smiled down at her, and they gazed into each other's eyes as if the crowded chamber, the whole world, had vanished but for the two of them.

A cold sadness washed over Celia at the sight. She had once looked at John like that, sure that he felt that incandescent connection too. But it had been false in the end.

She turned away from the sight of Anton and Rosamund and pretended to study the tapestry on the wall. But the vivid greens and reds of the silken threads blurred in her vision, and she saw only that long-ago summer day. The sun so bright and warm in a cloudless azure sky, the cool shadows under the ancient oak tree where she'd waited for him. Imagining his kisses, the embrace of his strong body…

But he had not come, even after he'd hinted at a future with her. The warm sun had melted away and there had been only the shadows.

It was not him, she told herself fiercely. He was not here. Not now.

The door swung open again, and this time it was the Queen's major-domo. A tense hush fell over the crowd.

Celia turned around to face him, wiping fiercely at her eyes. She hadn't cried in three years. She could not start now.

"Mistress Celia Sutton, Her Grace will see you now," the man announced.

Bitterly envious looks spun towards Celia, but she ignored them and slowly made her way forward. This was her chance. She couldn't let the memory of John Brandon distract her for even an instant. He had taken too much from her already.

Just inside the door a small looking glass hung on the wall, and she glimpsed her reflection there—the black cap on her smooth, tightly pinned dark hair, the high fur collar of her gown, the jet earrings in her ears. In mourning for a husband she could not truly mourn.

Her face looked chalk-white with worry, just like everyone else's in that room outside, but red streaked her cheekbones as if in memory of that long-ago summer's day. Her grey eyes glowed with unshed tears.

She forced them away, clasping her hands tightly before her waist as she followed the major-domo into the inner sanctum of the privy chamber. It was also crowded there, but the atmosphere was lighter, the conversation free of the strained quality outside. Ladies-in-waiting in their pale silks sat on cushions and low stools scattered over the floor and around the marble fireplace, whispering and laughing over their embroidery. Handsome young courtiers played cards in the corner, casting flirtatious glances at the ladies.

But the Queen's most favourite of all, Robert Dudley, was nowhere to be seen. Everyone said that after the alarming events of the Christmas season, the attempts on the Queen's life, he worked day and night to ensure the security of the palace. Nor was the Queen's chief secretary, Lord Burghley, who so rarely left her side, in evidence.

Queen Elizabeth sat by herself next to the window, a table covered with the scrolls of petitions beside her. The pale grey sunlight filtered through the thick glass, turning her red-gold hair into a fiery halo and making her fair ivory skin glow. She wore a splendourous robe of crimson velvet trimmed with white fur over a gold silk gown, rubies on her fingers and in her ears, and a band of pearls holding back her hair.

She looked every inch the young Sun Queen, but her dark eyes were shadowed and the set of her mouth was grim, as if the events of the last few days had taken their toll on her.

Celia had heard that those strange occurrences were not the Queen's only worries. Parties from Austria and Sweden were at Whitehall to press their marriage suits. Spain and France were constant threats. And the Queen's cousin to the north, Mary Queen of Scots, was always a thorn in Elizabeth's side.

It was almost enough to make Celia feel her own troubles were tiny in comparison! No one was trying to kill her *or* marry her.

"Mistress Sutton," Queen Elizabeth said. "You have had a long wait, I fear."

Celia curtsied low and made her way to the Queen's desk. Elizabeth tapped her long pale fingers on the papers, her rings sparkling. "I'm just grateful Your Grace has the time to meet with me."

Elizabeth waved her words away. "You may not be so grateful when you hear what I have to say, Mistress Sutton. Please sit."

A footman leaped forward with a stool, and Celia sank onto it gratefully. She had a terrible feeling this interview would not go as she so fervently wished. "Briony Manor, Your Grace?"

"Aye." Elizabeth held up a scroll. "It seems clear to us that your grandfather's wish was for the estate to go to Master Gustavson's mother and then to him. We feel we cannot go against this."

Celia felt that chill wash over her again—the cold of disappointment, of an anger she had to suppress. If she could not go to Briony, where *could* she go? What would be her home? "Yes, Your Grace."

"I am sorry," Elizabeth said, and there was a tinge of true regret in her voice. She even used "I" instead of the official "we". "When I was a girl, I had no true place of my own. No place where I could be assured of my own security. Everything I had was dependent on others—my father, my brother, my sister. Even my life depended on their whims."

Celia glanced at the Queen in surprise. Elizabeth so seldom spoke of the difficult past. Why would she now, and to Celia of all people? "Your Grace?"

"I know how you must feel, Mistress Sutton. We are alike in some ways, I think. And that is why I sense that I can ask a great favour of you."

Ask? Or demand? "I will do anything I can to serve Your Grace, of course."

Elizabeth tapped at the papers again. "You have heard the recent rumours surrounding my cousin Queen Mary, I am sure. She always seems of such acute interest to my courtiers."

"I—well, aye, Your Grace. I sometimes hear tales of Queen Mary. Is there a specific rumour you refer to?"

Elizabeth laughed. "Oh, yes, there *are* many. But I refer to the fact that she intends to marry again. They say she has hopes of a union equal to her first with the King of France. I hear she has her sights set on Don Carlos of Spain—King Phillip's son."

"I have heard such rumours as well, Your Grace," Celia said. She had also heard Don Carlos was a violent lunatic, but even a reputed great beauty like Queen Mary seemed willing to overlook that for the chance to be Queen of Spain.

Elizabeth suddenly slammed her fist down on the desk, sending an inkwell clattering to the floor. "That cannot be! My cousin cannot make such a powerful alliance. She is menace enough as it is. I have suggested she should marry an English nobleman. I must have someone I can trust in her Court."

"Your Grace?" Celia said in confusion. How could she assist in such a task?

Elizabeth lowered her voice to a whisper. "I have a plan, you see, Mistress Sutton. But I will need help to see it carried off."

"How can I help, Your Grace? I know of no candidates for Queen Mary's hand."

"Oh, I will take care of that, Mistress Sutton. I have the perfect candidate in mind—someone I can trust completely. I cannot say who just yet, but I promise you will know all you need to soon." The Queen sat back in her chair and reached for one of the papers on her desk. "In the meantime my cousin, the Countess of Lennox, who is Mary's cousin as well, petitions for her son Lord Darnley to be given a passport to visit his father who is now resident in Edinburgh."

Celia nodded. She knew well of the Countess's petition, as Lady Lennox had made certain indiscreet confidences to her in the last few days. Lady Lennox hoped that once Queen Mary met Lord Darnley, who was tall, blond and angelically handsome, she would marry him and make him King of Scotland. His own royal lineage would strengthen Mary's claim to be Elizabeth's heir.

Celia was not so sure such a plan could work, hinging as it did on Lord Darnley. Even she could see, from her brief time at Court, that he was a drunken braggart under his pretty exterior, and rather too fond of men.

"Yes, Your Grace," she said.

"It appears Lady Lennox has made a friend of you in these last few days."

"Lady Lennox has been welcoming to me. But she tells me little except that she misses her husband."

"I have been reluctant to let Lord Darnley travel north," Elizabeth said. "He seems the sort it is best to keep an eye on. But Lord Burghley counsels, and I concur, that we should allow him this passport now. He will depart for Scotland in a week's time."

"So soon, Your Grace?" Celia was surprised anyone could travel now. It was the coldest winter anyone could remember, with the Thames frozen through. Sensible people stayed home by their fires.

"I think time is imperative in this matter," the Queen said. "And Lord Darnley seems eager to go. I wish for you, Mistress Sutton, to be one of the travel party."

Celia tried not to gape at the Queen like a country lackwit. She had no idea what to say or even how to calm her jumbled thoughts. She—go to Scotland? "I fear I do not quite understand how I could help you in Edinburgh, Your Grace."

Elizabeth gave an impatient sigh. "You will serve Queen Mary as a lady-in-waiting—a gift from me. I need a lady's close eye on matters there, Mistress Sutton. Men are all very well for certain things, of course, and Burghley will have his spies in the party. But a woman sees things men are blind to—especially when it comes to other women. I need to know Mary's true thoughts concerning her possible marriage. And I need to know if she is…persuadable in that regard."

"And you believe I can do that?" Celia said carefully.

Elizabeth laughed. "I am sure you can. I have been watching you these last few days, Mistress Sutton, and I see how you notice everything around you. How you observe and listen. I need someone like that. Not a preening Court peacock who sees nothing but the cut of their own coat. It is vital that I know everything my cousin does right now. The security of our northern borders depends on her marital choice."

Celia nodded. She knew how unpredictable the Scottish Queen could be. Everyone knew that. And Celia did watch and listen; it was the only way for a woman alone to survive. She also knew how limited her own choices were. With no money or estate of her own, and no husband or family to lean on, she was dependent on the Queen's favour.

Better that than the cold charity of her in-laws.

"You would be rewarded for your efforts, of course," the Queen said. "As soon as Queen Mary's marriage is settled satisfactorily and you have returned to our Court you shall have a marriage of your own. The finest I can arrange, I promise you, Mistress Sutton. And then you will be settled for life."

Celia would rather have an estate of her own than another husband. In her experience husbands were useless things. But for now she would take what the Queen offered—and renegotiate later.

"What would be a—a satisfactory settlement?" she asked.

Elizabeth smiled and slid a folded letter from under the ledger on her desk to give to Celia. "This will tell you all you need to know, Mistress Sutton. I intend to propose my own marital candidate to Mary. When you have messages to send to me, you may give them to my own trusted contact and he will see they reach me quickly."

Celia tucked the letter into her velvet sleeve. "Contact, Your Grace?"

"Aye. You can meet him now." Elizabeth gestured to the major-domo, who bowed and disappeared through a door tucked into the panelling. He returned in only a moment, followed by a tall, lean man clad in fashionable black and tawny velvet and satin.

John Brandon. It *was* him she had seen before. He was no illusion. Celia half rose at the sight of him, and then fell back onto her stool. She felt cold all over again.

His eyes—those bright sky-blue eyes she had once loved so much—widened when they glimpsed her. For a fleeting instant she saw a flare of emotion in their depths. A hint of a smile touched his lips. But a veil quickly fell over those eyes, and she could read nothing there but fashionable boredom. He gave no signs of recognising her at all.

"Ah, Sir John, there you are," Queen Elizabeth said. She waved him forward, holding out her hand for him to bow over. He gave her an elaborate salute and a flirtatious grin that made her laugh.

"Your Grace outshines the sun itself," he said. "Even in the midst of the winter you send us warmth and light."

"Flatterer," the Queen said, laughing even harder.

Celia remembered that smile all too well, and how it also had made *her* laugh and blush whenever he turned it in her direction. Back then it had been half hidden in a close-cropped beard. Now he was clean-shaven, the sharp, elegant angles of his chiselled face revealed and the full force of that smile unleashed.

From the corner of her eye Celia saw some of the young ladies-in-waiting sigh and giggle. Yes, she remembered very well that feeling—that sense of melting under the heat of his smile. But that had been long ago, and she had learned the painful consequences of falling under John Brandon's spell.

"Sir John, this is Mistress Celia Sutton, who will also be journeying to Scotland," Queen Elizabeth said. She lowered her voice to whisper confidentially, "She will give you any messages to be dispatched directly to me. You must see that she stays safe in Edinburgh."

A frown flickered over John's face, as if he was not happy with the task. But he could not be any less happy than Celia. Her heart sank in appalled confusion. She would have to travel with *him*? Confide in *him*?

She had the wild impulse to leap from her seat, cry out that she refused the Queen's task and run from the room. But she forced herself to stay where she was, biting her lip until she tasted blood to keep from shouting. She could not refuse the Queen. There was nowhere for her to run.

John's frown vanished as quickly as Celia had glimpsed it. He bowed again and said, "I am Your Grace's servant in all things," he said.

Elizabeth leaned back in her chair with a smug little cat's smile. "Come now, Sir John. This is surely far from the most onerous task I have asked of you. Mistress Sutton is quite pretty, is she not? I'm sure spending time with her will not be so difficult on your long journey."

Celia froze at the Queen's teasing words. John's glance flickered over her with not much interest. "I fear that when Your Grace is near I can see nothing else," he said.

Elizabeth laughed. "Nevertheless, I expect the two of you will work together very well. Your mother was Scottish, was she not, Sir John?"

A muscle tightened along John's jaw. "Yes, Your Grace."

"She even lived at the Court of Queen Mary's mother, when Marie of Guise was Regent, I believe?" Elizabeth said carelessly, as if those years when the English and Scottish armies under Queen Marie de Guise had been at bitter war was a mere trifle. "So you should be able to assist Mistress Sutton in learning the ways of the Scottish Court. Perhaps you will even rediscover your own family there."

"I have no family but that of England, Your Grace," he said tightly.

Elizabeth waved this away and said, "You may both leave us now. You will have a great many tasks to prepare for your journey, and I must finish these petitions before tonight's banquet."

Celia rose slowly from her stool and curtsied, her legs trembling and unsteady. She still could not quite believe all that happened in this strange short meeting. Her worries of having no home or income had been whisked away, only to be replaced by the sudden reappearance of John Brandon and a journey to Scotland to spy on Queen Mary. Her head spun with it all.

She would have laughed if it was not so coldly serious.

John bowed to the Queen, and the major-domo came forward again to lead them away. He took them not to the crowded presence chamber but through a hidden door into a small, dimly lit closet. After the brightness of the privy chamber Celia could see nothing but the shadow of heavy tapestries on dark wood walls.

She rubbed her hand over her eyes and took a deep breath. When she looked again the servant was gone— and she was alone with John.

He watched her closely, his lean, muscled shoulders tense and his handsome face wiped of all expression.

"Hello, Celia," he said quietly. "It has been a long time, has it not?"

Chapter Two

Celia stared up at John in the shadows of the closet. The faint, hazy bars of light fell over his face, and she saw that the years had changed him just as they had her. He was leaner, harder, his eyes a wintry, icy blue as they studied her warily.

Once she had thought those eyes as warm as a summer sky, melting her heart, piercing all her defences. But now her heart was a stone, a heavy weight within her that was numb to all feeling. It was better this way. Feelings were deceptive, treacherous. Never to be trusted.

Especially when it came to this man.

Celia stepped back until she felt the hard wood panelling of the wall against her shoulders. He didn't move, yet his eyes never wavered from her face and it felt as if he followed her. It felt as if he pressed up against her in that dim, quiet light, his hard, hot body touching her as it once had. Demanding a response from her.

She twisted her hands into her skirts, struggling not to look away from him. Not to show her weakness.

"Aye, it *has* been a long while," she said, once she finally found her voice again.

The last time she'd seen him he had been kissing her beneath that tree, their secret meeting place. His body had held her against the rough wood of the trunk, just as she braced herself to the wall now. He had kissed her, his mouth and tongue claiming hers, demanding she give him all her response as he dragged her skirt up, baring her to his touch. There had been such a wild desperation between them that day, a need such as she had never known. He had made her dream of a romantic, glorious future with him.

And the next day he was gone. Vanished without a word.

"Yet not nearly long enough," she said coldly. "I thought never to see you again."

His glance swept down over her again, taking in her austere gown, her ringless fingers, the tight, smooth twist of her hair. For an instant another image flashed in her mind. John taking her hair down, freeing it from its pins and running his hands through its heavy length. Calling it a fairy queen's hair as he buried his face in it…

Those all-seeing blue eyes focused on her face again, narrowing as he watched her closely, as if seeking her thoughts. Once she had gifted him with all she was, given herself to him in every way.

She hoped she was no longer such a fool. She looked back at him with a steady, cool daring. Let him try to read her, play her again. The besotted, silly, giddy Celia he'd once known was gone. John had killed her—with the able assistance of her wretched husband and foolish brother.

"I've thought of you, Celia," he said.

She quickly scrambled to cover her surprise at his words. He had *thought* of her? Surely not. Unless it had been to chuckle at her naivety. The country girl who had fallen so easily for his charm, his dalliance to pass the time of rural exile.

Celia laughed. "I would have thought Court life would be far too busy for any idle nostalgia, John. So many tournaments to win, ladies to woo. I'm sure every moment is filled for a man of your...assets."

She let her gaze drift down over his body—the long, lean line of his legs in his tall leather boots, the snake-like hips and powerful shoulders. The years had not softened him one bit.

Her stare slid over the bulge in his breeches and she had to turn away. She remembered that part of him all too well...hot velvet over steel, sliding against her, inside of her.

"Aye," she said tightly. "You must be busy indeed."

Something seemed to crack in his iron control then. As fast as the strike of a hawk diving for its prey he seized her arms in his hard hands and held her against the wall. Those blue eyes she had thought so icy burned down at her in a white-hot blaze.

Celia could feel her own carefully built walls slipping and she struggled to hold onto them. Nay, this could not be happening! Five minutes in John's presence could not be destroying all she had built up to protect herself. She twisted away from him but he wouldn't let her go.

"Let me go!" she cried. His hands just tightened, holding her between the wall and his body. The heat of him, the vital, fiery *life* that had always been a part of him, wrapped around her like velvety unbreakable bonds. She remembered the tenderness, the need she had once felt with him.

"What has happened to you, Celia?" he said roughly.

"What do you mean?" she gasped.

She went very still and stared at the hard angle of his jaw above the high collar of his doublet. A muscle flexed there and his lips were pressed in an angry line. She imagined twisting her hands in that collar, tighter and tighter, until he let her go. Until she could hurt him as he had once hurt her.

"You look like the Celia I remember," he said. One hand slid slowly down her arm, rubbing her velvet sleeve over her skin until he touched her bare wrist. Something flared in his eyes as he felt the leap of her pulse, and he twined his fingers with hers.

Celia was too frozen to pull away. She felt like the hawk's prey in truth, mesmerised as he swooped closer and closer.

"You're even more beautiful than you were then," he said, his voice softer and deeper. "But your eyes are hard."

Celia jerked in his arms. "You mean I am not a foolish, gullible girl who can be lured by a man's pretty words? I have learned my lesson well since we last met, John, and I'm grateful for it."

He raised the hand he held to study her fingers. The pale skin and neat buffed nails. His thumb brushed over her bare ring finger. Celia tried to twist out of his caress, but despite his deceptive gentleness he held her fast.

"You aren't married?" he asked.

"Not any longer," she answered with a bitter laugh. "Thanks to God's mercy. And I intend never to be again."

He raised her hand, and to her shock pressed his mouth to the hollow of her palm. His lips were parted, and she could feel the moist heat of him moving slowly over her skin. It made her legs tremble, her whole treacherous body go weak, and she braced herself tighter against the wall.

That weakness, that rush of need she had thought she was finished with, made her angry. She made herself go stiff and unyielding, building her defensive walls up again stone by hard-won stone.

"I may have changed, John, but you certainly have not," she said coldly. "You still take what you want with no thought for anyone else. A conquering warrior who discards whatever no longer amuses you."

His mouth froze on her skin. Slowly he raised his head and his stare met hers. She almost gasped at the raw, elemental fury she saw in those depths. The blue had turned almost black, like the power of a summer storm.

"You know nothing of me," he whispered, and it was all the more forceful for its softness. "Nothing of what I have had to do in my life."

I know you left me! her mind cried out. Left her to the cruel hands of her husband, to a life where she had nowhere to turn for sanctuary. She bit down on her lip to keep from shouting the words aloud.

"I know I do not want to work with you on the Queen's business," she said.

"No more than I want to work with you," he answered. With one more hard glance down her body, he abruptly let her go and spun away from her. His back and shoulders were rigid as he raked his hands through his hair. "But the Queen has commanded it. Would you go against her orders?"

Celia braced her palms against the wall, trying to still the primitive urge to smooth the light brown waves of his hair where he had tousled them. "Of course I would not go against the Queen."

"Then to Edinburgh we go," he said.

He heaved in a deep breath, and Celia could practically see his armour lowered back into place. He shot her a humourless smile over his shoulder.

"I shall see you at the ball tonight, Celia."

She watched him leave the small closet, the door clicking shut behind him. She was surrounded by heavy silence, pressing in on her from every corner until she nearly screamed from it.

She let herself slide down the wall until she sat in the puddle of her skirts. Her head was pounding, and she let it drop down into her hands as she struggled to hold back the tears.

She had thought her life could become no worse, no more complicated. But she had been wrong. Sir John Brandon was the greatest, most terrible complication of all.

* * *

God's blood. Celia Sutton.

John shoved the pile of documents away so violently that many of them fluttered to the floor, and slumped back in his chair. It was of vital importance that he read all of them, that he knew exactly what he would be up against in Scotland, yet all he could see, all he could think about, was Celia.

Celia. Celia.

He raked his fingers hard through his hair, but she wouldn't be dislodged from his mind. Those cool grey eyes watching him in the shadows of that closet, sliding down his body as if she was remembering exactly what he was remembering himself.

The hot touch of bare skin to bare skin, mouths and hands exploring, tasting.

Her keening cries as he entered her, joined with her more deeply and truly than he ever had with anyone before. Or since.

But then her regard had changed in an instant, becoming hard and distant, cold as the frozen Thames outside his window. His Celia—the woman whose secret memory had sustained him for so long, despite everything—was gone.

Or maybe she was just hidden, buried behind those crossed swords he'd seen in this new, hard Celia's eyes. It was clear she had walled herself away from something, that her soul had been deeply wounded, and no matter what they had once been to each other she wouldn't let him reach her now. And she was quite right. One of those wounds on her soul had been placed there by him.

Once he had wanted her more than anything else in the world. She had awakened things in him he had thought he could never feel. He had even dared to dream of a future with her for one brief, bright moment. That connection was still there, after all these years. When he'd touched her it had been as if he could sense her thoughts, her fury, her passion. Hatred so close to lust he'd almost tasted it, because it had called out to the yearnings he felt just as strongly.

It had taken every ounce of his iron control not to push her to the floor, shove her skirts above her waist, raise her hips in his hands and drive his tongue into her. Taste her, feel her, until her walls fell and his Celia was with him again. The girl who had once made him smile.

He groaned as he felt the tightness in his codpiece, half-hard ever since he'd first touched her, lengthen. Just the memory of how she tasted, like summer honey, the way she would drive her fingers into his hair and pull him closer between her legs, had him aroused.

But if the murderous look in her eyes was any indication, memories were as close as he would ever get to *that* part of her again.

John pushed himself up from his chair and strode over to the window of his small chamber. He opened the casement to let the freezing wind rush over him, despite the fact that he had discarded his doublet and wore only a thin linen shirt. He needed the cold to remind him of his task, his duty. He had never failed in his service to the Queen. He couldn't fail now, no matter how much Celia distracted him.

He could see the river, a frozen silver ribbon as grey and icy as Celia's eyes. This Christmas season had been the coldest anyone could remember, so frigid the Thames had frozen solid and a frost fair was set up on the surface. It had warmed a bit in the quiet days after the Christmas revels, but chunks of ice still floated along the water and the people who dared to go outside were muffled in cloaks and scarves.

And he would have to travel to Scotland in the cold— and take Celia with him. Long days huddled together for heat, nights in secluded inns, bound together in danger and service to Queen Elizabeth. Surely there she would open to him? Surely there he could destroy all her shields, one by one, until his Celia was revealed to him again?

Nay! John cracked his palm down hard on the windowsill, splintering the cold brittle wood. This journey was meant to neutralise the constant threat of Queen Mary and her possible marriage alliances, not to be a chance for him to lose himself in Celia all over again. To dream of what he could never have. He had to remember that always.

Any chance he and Celia had ever had was long lost.

A knock sounded at the door.

"Enter!" John barked, louder than he'd intended. His temper was on edge and he had to rein it in.

But he hadn't completely concealed his anger when his friend Lord Marcus Stanville came into the room, caught a glimpse of John's face, and raised his dark golden brow.

"Perhaps I should come back another time," Marcus said. "If I don't want my nose bashed in by your fist."

John grinned reluctantly and shook his head. He sat back down in his chair and rubbed at the back of his neck. "The ladies of the Court would never forgive me if I ruined your pretty face."

Marcus gave an answering grin and shook back the long, tawny mane the ladies also loved. If they hadn't been friends since childhood, fostered in the same household after their parents died, John would surely hate the popinjay.

Yet he knew that the handsome face concealed a devious mind and a quick sword arm. They had saved each other's lives more than once.

"They *do* seem terribly fond of my visage just as it is," Marcus said, carelessly sprawling out in the other chair. "But a judiciously placed wound or two might elicit some sympathy in the heart of a certain lady…"

"Lady Felicity again?"

"Aye. She's a hard-hearted wench."

John laughed. "You just aren't accustomed to chasing. Usually women throw themselves under your feet for a mere smile."

Marcus gave a snort. "Says the man who has every woman in London lining up for his bed."

John scowled as he remembered Celia's grey eyes, cold as the winter sky when she looked at him. "Not every woman," he muttered.

"What? Never say a lady has refused Sir John Brandon! Have pigs been seen flying over London Bridge? Has Armageddon arrived?"

John threw a heavy book at Marcus's laughing head. Marcus merely ducked and tossed it right back.

"I never thought to see this day," Marcus said. "No wonder you looked so thunderstruck."

"Enjoy it while you can," John said. "For soon enough we will be on our way to bloody freezing Edinburgh."

Marcus grew sombre. "Aye, so we will. 'Tis not an assignment I relish, playing nursemaid to that drunken lordling lout Darnley. I wager the devil himself couldn't keep *him* out of trouble."

"I think there is more to this journey than that," John said.

Marcus sat forward in his chair, his hands braced on his knees. "You've talked to Burghley, then?"

"Not as yet, but I'm sure we will be summoned tomorrow."

"Will it be like our journey to Paris?"

John remembered Paris and what had happened there. The deceptions and danger. The sorrow over what had happened with Celia. "The Scottish Queen is always a thorn in Elizabeth's side."

"And will we have to pluck it out?"

"I fear so. One way or another." All while John dealt with his own thorn—one with the softest, palest skin beneath her barbs. "The Queen is sending someone else to Edinburgh as well."

Marcus groaned. "As well as Darnley and his cronies?"

"Aye. Mistress Celia Sutton." Even saying her name, feeling it on his tongue, twisted something deep inside him. Those tender feelings he had once had for her haunted him now.

"Celia Sutton?" Marcus said, his eyes widening. "She could freeze a man's balls off just with a look."

John gave a harsh laugh as he remembered the erection that had only just subsided. An almost painful hardness just from her look, her touch. The smell of her skin. "She is to be the Queen's own emissary—a representative to show Elizabeth's affections to her cousin."

"She might as well have sent a poisoned ring, then," Marcus scoffed. "Though there is something about Mistress Sutton that seems…"

His voice trailed away, and his eyes sharpened with speculation as he looked at John.

John held up his hand. "Do not even say it."

They had been friends so long that Marcus obviously saw the warning in John's face. He shrugged and pushed himself to his feet.

"Your passions are your own business, John," he said, "no matter how strange. Just as mine are. And now I must go and dress for the Queen's ball. I have little time left to woo Lady Felicity before we leave for hell."

Marcus strode from the room, leaving John alone to his brooding thoughts again. He looked back outside, to where the cold winter night was quickly closing in. Torches flickered along the banks of the river, the only light in the cloud-covered city.

It felt as if he was already in hell. He had been for

three years—ever since he'd betrayed Celia and thus lost her for ever. The only woman he could have dared to envisage a future with had been her.

Chapter Three

Celia stared at her reflection in the small looking glass as the maidservant brushed and plaited her hair before pinning it up in a tightly wound knot. She was even gladder now that the Queen had given her a rare, precious private chamber, away from anyone else's prying eyes and gossiping tongues. Anyone looking at her now would surely see the agitation in her eyes, the way she could not keep her hands still.

She twisted them harder in her lap, buried them in the fur trim of her robe. She had to go down to the ball soon, and there she would have to smile and talk as if nothing was amiss. She would have to listen and watch, to learn all she could about the hidden reasons for this sudden journey to Edinburgh. She had to be wary and cautious as always, careful of every step.

She closed her eyes, suddenly so weary. She had been cautious every day, every minute, for three years. Would the rest of her life be like this? She was very much afraid it would. Thomas Sutton was dead, but the taut wariness was still there. The certainty of pain.

In an unconscious gesture she rubbed at her shoulder. It was long healed, but sometimes she could vow she still felt it. She had fought so hard for control. She would not lose it now. Not because of *him*.

Behind her closed eyes she saw John Brandon's face, half in mysterious shadow as he held her to the wall, his blue eyes piercing through her like a touch, as if he saw past her careful armour to everything she kept hidden. His hands on her had roused so much within her—things she'd thought long-dead and buried, things she'd thought she could never feel again because her marriage had killed them in her.

One look from John scared her more than any of Thomas's blows ever could. Because Thomas had not known her, had never possessed her. Not really. She had always hidden her true self from him even as he'd tried to beat it from her. But John had once possessed all of her, everything she had to offer, and because of him it was gone now.

"Are you quite well, Mistress Sutton?" she heard the maid ask, bringing her back to the present moment.

Celia opened her eyes and gave the girl a polite smile. "Just a bit of a headache. It will soon pass."

"Shall I loosen your hair a bit, then? A style of loose curls here and here is quite fashionable."

Celia studied herself in the looking glass. Her hair was already dressed as it always was, the heavy black waves tightly plaited and pinned in a knot at the nape of her neck. Since it was a ball, a beaded black caul covered the knot, but that was its only decoration. It was all part of the armour.

"Nay, this will do," she said, slipping on her jet and pearl earrings. "I will dress now."

She eased out of her robe and let the maid help her into her gown: a bodice and overskirt of black velvet with a stomacher and petticoat of glossy purple brocade trimmed with jet beads. Her sleeves were also black, tied with purple ribbons. Even her shoes and the garters that bound her white silk stockings were black.

Thomas had been dead for many months. She could put aside mourning and wear colours again, the blues and greens she had once loved, but she liked the reminder of where she had been. Where she vowed never to be again. The half-world of mourning suited her.

Celia held up her arm for the maid to lace on the tight sleeves and pluck bits of the white chemise between the ribbons. As she stared at the fireplace she let herself drift away, just for a moment, and remember when she first met John.

She'd been just a silly girl then, who had never been to Court, never away from her family and their country gentry neighbours. John Brandon had been sent to stay with his uncle at a nearby estate, exiled from Court for some unknown scandal. He'd been meant to rusticate until he had learned his lesson and repented.

That dark hint of some roguish secret had made her cousins all afire with speculation even before they'd met him, and Celia had not been immune to it. She'd liked to sit by the fire of a winter evening and listen to romantic tales as much as any young lady, and a handsome rake from London seemed a perfect part of such stories. Then, when she had seen him at last, a glimpse across his uncle's hall at a banquet...

It had been as if the whole world tipped upside down and everything looked completely different. His eyes, his smile, the way he strode through the crowd right to her side and kissed her hand—she'd been dazzled.

Celia shook her head hard now as she remembered. *Foolish, foolish girl.*

And now foolish woman. For hadn't she almost melted all over again when he touched her today?

But the next time they met, touched, *she* would be the one in control. She had to be.

As soon as the maid had finished adjusting her gown she fastened a black feather fan and a silver pomander to the chain girdle at her waist. As she had no sword, they would have to do.

But when the maid turned away she bent and gathered up her skirts to tuck a small dagger in the sheath at her garter. She could not go down there completely unarmed.

As she made her way down the many staircases and along the twisting corridors of the palace the crowd grew thicker the closer she came to the great hall. After the nightly revels of Christmas Celia would have thought the courtiers would be weary of Queen Elizabeth's glittering displays, but there was a hum of excitement in the air, in the buzz of laughter and chatter around her as she was swept along.

She could hear music—the lively strains of a galliard—and the thunderous pattern of dancing feet. All around her was the rustle of fine satins, the flash of jewels, the smell of expensive perfumes, warm skin and wine. It all made her head spin, but she was caught in the tide now and could not get away. She was swept inexorably into the hall.

She slid her way through the crowd to a spot near one of the tapestry-hung walls, a little apart from all the frantic laughter, the jostling for position. She couldn't breathe when she was caught in the very midst of it all, buffeted by so many touches, so much desperate energy.

She took a goblet of wine from one of the servants in the Queen's livery and sipped at the rich red French wine as she studied the gathering. She prayed John would not be there, would not see her. She had barely recovered her hard-won composure after their last meeting. His body close to hers, his heat and scent in that dark closet…

Celia took a long gulp of the wine, and then another. She usually only drank small beer, slowly, always remembering what a monster drink had made of her husband. How it had destroyed her father after what had happened to her poor brother. But tonight she needed every fortification she could find.

As the wine warmed her blood she examined the company. The Queen led the dancing with her handsome Robert Dudley, who was now the Earl of Leicester, reputedly to make him of a stature worthy to be the Queen of Scots's consort. Queen Elizabeth's red-gold hair shimmered brighter than her gold brocade gown as she laughed and leaped, twirling higher and lighter than everyone else. The troubles of the last few weeks, and the troubles sure to come, seemed forgotten in the music and merriment.

Celia's gaze trailed over the Countess of Lennox, a great, large woman in black who stood near another wall and studied the revels with her lips pressed tightly together. She gave Celia a quick nod before turning to her son. Lord Darnley sulked and drank by her side, though even Celia knew he would not be there long. He could not stay away from his debauched pleasures for more than an hour.

He was handsome, Celia would admit that—very tall and lean, with golden hair and fine Tudor features. But, like his mother's, his mouth had a cruel cast that Celia recognised all too well. She didn't trust him, and she didn't know what game Queen Elizabeth played with him, Leicester and Mary.

She definitely did not know why *she* had to be involved in the messy quagmire. But beggars could not be choosers.

"Good evening to you, cousin." She heard a deep, quiet voice, lightly touched with a Scandinavian accent, behind her.

She turned to face the very man she had once blamed for that beggaring: her cousin Anton Gustavson. They had never known each other; his mother—her father's sister—had married a Swedish nobleman and disappeared to the frozen north before Celia was born. Then he'd appeared here at Court, with a party sent to woo the Queen on behalf of the Swedish King—and to claim a family estate Celia had hoped to have for her own. The last remnant of her family's lost fortune.

She had blamed Anton bitterly for this final disappointment. But now, as she looked into his wary dark eyes, she could no longer blame him. He sought his own redemption here in England, and perhaps he had found it with his new estate and his Lady Rosamund.

Celia still had to find hers.

"And good evening to you, too—cousin," she said. "Where is Lady Rosamund? Everyone says you two are quite inseparable of late."

"Not entirely so," Anton said. He gestured towards the dance floor, now a whirling stained-glass mosaic of brilliant jewels and silks. "She is dancing with Lord Marcus Stanville."

Celia saw that Rosamund did indeed dance with Lord Marcus, their two golden heads close together as he whirled her up into the air.

"Lord Marcus Stanville—one of the greatest flirts at Court," Celia said as she finished her wine and exchanged the empty goblet for a full one. "I'm surprised."

Anton laughed. "Rosamund is immune to his blandishments."

"But not to yours?"

He arched his dark brow at her. "Nay. Not to mine. We are soon to be married."

Celia swallowed hard on her sip of wine and carefully studied the dancers. A cold, hard knot pressed inside her, low and aching. Once she'd had the foolish hope she could marry someone she loved too.

"My felicitations to you, cousin," she said. "Surely you did not expect quite so much here when you left Sweden?"

"I had hoped to find family here," Anton said. "And you and I are all that is left. Can we not cry pax and be friends?"

Celia studied him over the silver rim of her goblet. Aye, he *was* her family. All she had. For an instant she thought she glimpsed a resemblance to her father in his eyes, and that hard knot inside her tightened. How she missed her family sometimes. She was so alone without them.

"Pax, cousin," she said, and slowly held out her hand to him.

Anton gave a relieved laugh and bowed over her hand. "You are most welcome at our home at any time, Celia."

Celia shook her head. "You needn't worry, Anton. I shall not be the dark fairy at the feast. The Queen is sending me on an errand, and I probably shan't be back for some time."

A frown flickered over his face. "What sort of errand?"

Celia opened her mouth to give some vague answer, but she stopped at a sudden sensation of heat on the back of her neck. She pressed her fingers over the spot, just below the tight twist of her hair, and shivered.

She glanced over her shoulder and met John Brandon's bright blue eyes staring right at her. Burning. His head tilted slightly to one side, as if he was considering her, as if she was a puzzle, then he moved towards her.

Celia reacted entirely on instinct. She shoved her empty goblet into Anton's hand and said, "Excuse me. I must go now."

"Celia, what…?" Anton said, his voice startled, but Celia was gone.

She only knew she had to run, to get away, before John could catch her and strip her soul bare with those eyes as he had come so close to doing earlier.

The hall was even more crowded and noisy than before, and Celia had to elbow her way past knots of people. She was a small woman, though, and slid past the worst of the crowds and into the corridor. She could still hear the high-pitched hum of voices, but it seemed muted and blurred, as sounds heard underwater. The air pressed in on her, hot and close.

Yet she could still vow she heard the soft, inexorable fall of his boots on the floor, coming closer.

"I am going mad," she whispered. She lifted the heavy hem of her skirts and hurried to the end of the corridor, where it turned onto another and then another. Whitehall was a great maze. It was quieter here, darker, the narrow, dim length lit at intervals by flickering torches set high in their sconces. She heard a soft giggle from behind one of the tapestries, a low male groan.

She didn't know which way to go, and that moment's hesitation cost her. She felt hard fingers close over her arm and spin her around.

She lost her footing and fell against a velvet-covered chest. Her hands automatically braced against that warm, solid wall and a diamond button pressed into her soft palm. It was John. She could smell him, knew his touch. The hawk had swooped down and caught its prey.

She forced herself to freeze, to go perfectly still and not panic and run again.

"Do you have an urgent appointment somewhere, Celia?" he asked quietly. "You certainly seem in a great hurry."

Celia tried carefully to move away from him, slide out of his hold on her arms, but it seemed she was not unobtrusive enough. His other arm came around her, a steel bar at her back.

She eased her hands down his chest, and that hold tightened and kept her where she was. Her head was tucked under his chin, and she could feel the strong, steady beat of his heart under her palm.

Her own heart was racing. She couldn't breathe too deeply because his scent was all around her. She closed her eyes and sought out the icy centre that had held her together all these years. The distance that had saved her. It was not there now. He had torn it away.

"I am tired," she said. "I merely sought to retire. There was no need to chase me down like this."

John gave a low, rough chuckle. "Usually when a woman runs like that she wants to be chased."

"Like a doomed deer on the Queen's hunt?" Celia choked out. She had been on such hunts, had seen Queen Elizabeth cut the fallen deer's heart out. Celia had thought she herself had no heart left to be ripped out. It seemed she was wrong. There was still one small, hidden part of it, bleeding, and he was dangerously close to touching it again.

John had surely chased scores of eager women since they had last met, and held them thus. Kissed them in the darkness until they happily bled for him too.

"I am not most women," she said, and tried once more to wrench out of his arms.

He only held her closer, until she felt her feet actually leave the floor. Lifting her in his arms, he carried her backwards until she felt the cold stone wall at her back, chilly through her brocade bodice.

Her eyes flew open to find he had carried her into a small window embrasure, where they were surrounded by darkness and silence.

"Nay," he said. "You, Celia Sutton, are quite unlike any other woman in all England." His voice held the strangest, most unreadable tone—bemused, angry.

"And you know all of them, I am sure," she muttered.

John laughed and eased her back another step. He braced his palms to the wall on either side of her head, holding her trapped by his body as he had earlier. "Your faith in my stamina is quite heartening, my fairy queen. But I have only had twenty-eight years on this earth. Alas, not long enough to find all the women out there."

Hearing his old name for her—*fairy queen*—once whispered in her ear as they embraced in a forest grove, snapped something inside Celia. He had no right to call her that. Not any longer.

Before she could think, her hand shot out and her fingers curled hard around his manhood.

He froze, and she heard the hiss of his indrawn breath. His eyes narrowed as he stared down at her, and the very air around them seemed to crackle with a new tension. This strange game, whatever it was, was shifting and changing.

The codpiece of his breeches was not a fashionably

elaborate one, and she could feel the outline of him through the fine velvet. He was already semi-erect, and as her fingers tightened he stirred and lengthened. Oh, yes, she did remember this—how he liked to be touched. Caressed. She felt her hard-won sense of control steal back over her.

She twisted her wrist to cradle the underside of his penis on her palm and slowly, slowly traced her way up. She remembered how it felt naked, hot satin over steel, the vein just there throbbing with his life force. She reached its base, and with another twist of her fingers she held his testicles.

"Is this what happens when you catch your prey, John?" she whispered. She stroked a soft caress, lightly scraping the edge of her thumbnail over him.

She could feel the burn of his eyes on her as he held himself rigid around her. For once *she* had caught *him* unbalanced. He didn't know which way she would jump. And neither did she. Not any longer. He did that to her.

She had acted on instinct, reaching out to bring her control back. But it seemed to be slipping even further away.

"Usually they get down on their knees to me and take me in their mouths about now," John said crudely.

One hand left the wall by her head and she felt his finger press lightly to her lower lip. He traced the soft skin there. The merest whisper of a touch.

Celia gasped, and he used that small movement to slide his finger into her mouth, over her tongue. She jerked her head back, but she could still taste him—salt and wine. She wished she could pull away from him and snatch her dagger from its sheath on her thigh, plunge it into his heart so he could not touch *her* heart again.

"That will never happen," she said.

"Nay? I think it will in my dreams tonight," John answered. "But perhaps you want me on my knees to *you* instead?"

Before she knew what he was doing, he'd deftly twisted out of her grasp and arched his body back from hers. The hand that had been at her mouth slid all the way down to her skirts and drew up the heavy fabric until her legs were bare. The white stockings glowed in the darkness.

As Celia watched in frozen shock he fell to his knees before her and let those skirts fall back over him. She tried to kick him away, but his strong hands closed over the soft, bare skin of her thighs above those stockings. He caressed her there, on the tender inner curve of her leg, and pressed her legs further apart.

Then she felt his hot breath soft on the vulnerable curve of her, light as a sigh, just before his tongue plunged inside.

God's blood. Her eyes slammed shut and her palms pressed hard to the wall at the trembling, burning rush of sensation that shot through her body. Oh, dear heaven, but she had forgotten how it felt when he did that!

Just as she had remembered how he liked to be touched, he remembered how she liked to be kissed *there*. He licked up—one languorous stroke, then another—before flicking at that tiny, hidden spot with the tip of his tongue. She felt herself contract at the pleasure, felt a rush of moisture trickle onto her inner thigh, and he groaned.

How she wanted him. How she had missed him, missed *this*, the feeling of being so wondrously, vitally alive. It had been so long. She had been dead inside for so long…

For just an instant she let herself feel it, let him pleasure her. This was *John*. The only man who had ever touched her heart. But then his hand closed hard on her thigh, just above the dagger, stroking her there so tenderly. So deceptively—just like before.

Before he'd destroyed her.

With a ragged sob she jerked herself away from him. She pulled her skirts from above his head and sent him toppling to the floor. But she also lost her own balance, and fell heavily on her hip against the wall. She leaned onto the cold stone for support and tried not to cry. Not to feel.

But his heat was still around her, and the musky scent of their arousal, the heated swirl of her feelings for him. She had to escape from it all.

John found his balance on his knees again, lithe as a cat. In the shadows she saw the frown on his face, the darkness of his eyes. He started towards her. "Celia…" he began.

But she stopped him with the sole of her shoe planted on his chest. She knew he could easily sweep any of her barriers away, yet he stayed where he was, watching her. She dug the heel of her shoe in, just enough to hold him there as she had with his balls in her hand.

"Celia, what has happened to you?" he said quietly.

She gave a hoarse, humourless laugh. How could she even begin to answer such a question? She gave him a slight push with her foot, and when he sat back on his heels she lurched upright to her feet. She ducked out of the hidden embrasure, and this time when she ran he did not follow.

Curse it all! Every instinct within John shouted at him to run after Celia, to catch her in his arms and hold her to him until she broke open and gave him all she had. All those dark secrets in her eyes. He wanted to strip away her clothes until she was naked before him, every pale, beautiful inch of her, and drive into her.

But he was too angry, and she was too brittle and fragile. She would surely shatter if he pushed her too hard, and the way he was feeling now he could not hold back. He braced his palms against the cold stone floor and let his head drop down, his eyes close as he struggled for control.

It was that damnable nickname. *Fairy queen.* His fairy queen. He could see her as she had been that day, her midnight-black hair loose over her bare shoulders, her grey-sky eyes gleaming an otherworldly silver as she looked up at him. She'd lain on a grassy, sunny spot in the woods, the light dappled over her skin, and John had never seen anyone so beautiful and free, so much a part of the nature around them. A fairy queen who had cast her magical spell over him. His wild youth had been forgotten when he saw her—the first time he'd felt such a rush of tenderness, dreamed of what he couldn't have. All because of her.

There seemed nothing of the fairy left in her now. She seemed instead an ice queen, encased in snow. But when she'd touched his manhood, when he'd tasted her, his Celia had flashed behind her cold eyes.

And, z'wounds, but she tasted the same as he remembered—of honey and dew. She had become wet when he'd kissed her there, the silken folds of her contracting over his tongue. Not so frozen after all. Did she remember too?

But still so far away from him. He remembered the panic in her eyes when she shoved him away, the way those walls in her eyes had slammed up again. It hurt to know she was so wary of him, even as he knew he so richly deserved it.

It was good she had run, for he obviously had no control at all when it came to her. Had he not resolved that very afternoon to stay away from her? To forget their past? Not to hurt her again, and not to torture himself with what he could no longer have? Only hours later he'd been on his knees under her skirt.

John pushed himself to his feet and automatically reached down to adjust his codpiece. He felt again her slender fingers on him, caressing him just where it was calculated to drive him insane. Pleasure and pain all mixed up in a blurred tangle.

When he emerged into the corridor Celia was long gone. The music from the ball floated back to him, echoing off the walls, mocking him with its merriment. He could feel someone watching him, and spun around to find Marcus leaning against a marble pillar with his arms crossed over his chest. He arched his brow at John.

"*Are* your balls frozen off, then?" Marcus asked with a grin.

John shot him an obscene gesture and turned to stride away down the corridor. His friend's laughter followed him.

It was certainly going to be a long and wretched journey to Edinburgh. Or were they all headed into hell instead?

Chapter Four

"Is this all of it, Mistress Sutton?" the maidservant asked as she fastened shut the travel chest.

Celia glanced around the small chamber. All of her black garments and his meagre personal possessions had been packed and carried away, and the box containing her few jewels and Queen Elizabeth's documents was tucked under her arm. She had no more excuses to linger.

"Yes, I think that is all," she said. She glanced in the looking glass. She wore a plain black wool skirt and velvet doublet for travel. Her hair was pinned up and held by a net caul and tall-crowned hat. She looked calm enough, composed and quiet, but part of her wanted to hide under the bed and not face the inevitable.

The past few days had passed in a blur of meetings with the Queen and Lord Burghley to learn more of her tasks in Scotland. She was to befriend Queen Mary, who was said to chatter freely with her favourite maids, and try to gauge her marital inclinations and re-

port back to Elizabeth. To try and persuade Mary that
an English marriage of her cousin's choosing would be
best for her. To watch and listen, which Celia had become very good at. A wary nature was always cautious
of what would happen next.

But Elizabeth said Mary should wed Lord Leicester,
and Burghley said Darnley. Celia wasn't sure whom to
incline Queen Mary towards—if the Scottish Queen
could be "inclined" at all.

There had also been banquets and balls, tennis games
to watch, and garden strolls, which she had tiptoed into
as if they were the flames of hell. But the chief demon,
John Brandon, had never appeared there to torment her.
To draw her into quiet corners and reveal parts of her
she had long ago encased in ice and buried. To watch
her with those eyes of his that saw too much.

She wasn't sure if she was grateful or angry he'd
stayed away.

No doubt he has much to occupy him, she thought
as she jerked on her leather riding gauntlets. Like saying farewell to all his *amours*.

Lord Burghley had said John would be her conduit in
Scotland for any messages, so she knew she would have
to face him eventually. Face what he had made her feel.

Celia stared down at the black leather over her palm
and remembered the hard heat of him in her hand. The
power and, yes, the pleasure she had felt in that one instant as he grew hard for her. The way she'd longed to
pull away his clothes and feel him against her again.
Part of her in every way.

She convulsed her hand into a fist. Maybe if she had

crushed him, hurt him, she would be done with him now—as he had once been done with her.

But the feeling of his mouth on her, driving her to a mad frenzy, told her they were not done with each other. Not at all.

She spun around and snatched up her riding crop, cutting it through the air with a sharp whistle. She imagined it was John's tight backside under the leather's touch, but pushed away that thought when a disturbing spasm of desire caught at her. The less she thought of John Brandon and his handsome body and sweet words the better!

Celia hurried downstairs and out through the doors into the courtyard, where the travelling party was assembling. It was chaos, the long line of horses and carts struggling into place as servants loaded last-minute bundles and trunks.

Lord Darnley and his mother stood slightly apart from the others as Lady Lennox whispered intently into his ear. He nodded sulkily, his gaze straying to where his chosen companions played at dice on the steps. Though it was early in the day, and long hours of travel awaited them, they were all obviously inebriated.

Celia was thankful that at least her tasks did not include being nursemaid to *them.* She would just as soon they fell off their horses and froze in a snow bank somewhere.

She studied the rest of the people. Servants piling onto the carts and courtiers unlucky enough to be chosen for this journey finding their horses. Lady Allison Parker, another of Elizabeth's ladies sent to cozen

Queen Mary, was letting one of Darnley's friends lift her into her saddle. She laughed as she settled her bright green skirts around her, flirtatiously letting the poor lad glimpse her long legs as her red hair gleamed in the greyish light.

Celia had the feeling she and Lady Allison would *not* become bosom bows on this journey.

Then she saw John, the merest flash of his light brown hair from the corner of her eye, and she stiffened. Every sense suddenly seemed heightened, the wind colder on her skin, the light brighter in her eyes.

She half turned to find that he stood near the front of the procession, holding the reins of a restless jet-black horse. He softly stroked the horse's nose, crooning in its ear, but his eyes were on Celia, intently focused. His body was held very still, as if he waited to see what she would do. Which way she would jump.

Celia remembered her fantasy of her riding crop on his backside, and she felt a smile tug at her lips. Her gaze flickered down to his long legs encased in leather riding breeches and tall black boots.

When she looked back to his face some unspoken promise seemed to burn in his eyes. As if he could see her thoughts, her fantasies, and he was only waiting to get her alone to make them come true.

Celia spun away from him, only to find that Lord Marcus Stanville watched her from the doorway. She had seen him talking with John a few times. Obviously they were friends. Celia was inclined to like Lord Marcus, with his golden good looks and light-hearted demeanour, but she did not like the way he watched her now. Like John, it was almost as if he could see what she was thinking and it amused him.

"An excellent day for a journey, wouldn't you say so, Mistress Sutton?" he said.

"If one enjoys freezing off one's vital appendages, mayhap," she answered tartly. "I would prefer staying by a warm fire, but perhaps you have different inclinations, Lord Marcus?"

He laughed, and Celia sensed John watching them. To her shock, Lord Marcus took her hand and raised it to his lips.

"I hope I am as adventurous as the next man, Mistress Sutton," he said, "but I confess some of the finest adventures of all can be had by a fire. Still, we must all do the Queen's bidding."

"Indeed we must," Celia said. "Whether we like it or not."

"I admit I was not overly enthusiastic about this task at first," Lord Marcus said. "But with you and my friend Brandon along it's looking more promising than an afternoon at the theatre."

Before Celia could demand he tell her what that meant, he took her elbow in his clasp and led her towards a waiting horse. He lifted her into the saddle and grinned up at her.

"Let the games begin, Mistress Sutton," he said.

Celia glanced at John, where he still stood several paces ahead of her. He watched her and Marcus with narrowed eyes, and Celia was sure the games had begun long ago.

And she had the terrible certainty that she was losing.

* * *

Celia stared out at the passing landscape as her horse plodded along, and tried not to rub at her numb thigh. They had been riding for several hours now, and the cold and boredom had conspired to put her in a sort of dream state. There was nothing before or after this steady forward movement, only the moment she was in.

And it gave her far too much time to think.

She wrapped the reins loosely around her gloved hands and watched the bare grey trees on either side of the road. The wind moaned through the skeletal branches, almost like low voices carrying her back into the past.

She tried not to look back at where she knew John was riding, but she was always very aware of him there. In the quiet that had fallen since the cold had driven everyone into silence, she fancied she could almost hear him as he shifted in his saddle or spoke in a low voice to Marcus.

Celia shook her head. It was going to be a very long journey. She needed to keep her focus on the task that awaited her in Edinburgh. And on the reward Queen Elizabeth would give her if she performed the task well—a rich marriage where she would never have to beg for her bread again.

A rich marriage to some nameless, faceless stranger, which she could only pray would be better than her first. It was her only choice now. She had to survive, to keep fighting.

And when she looked at John she feared she would lose the will to fight. He had always made her want to surrender to pure emotion, from the first moment she'd seen him. A shiver passed through her as she remembered how he'd taken her hand that first day, how he'd smiled down at her as if he already knew her.

"Cold, Mistress Sutton?" she heard him say.

For an instant his voice made her think she had been hurtled back in time. She blinked and glanced up, to find that while she had been woolgathering he'd drawn his horse up next to hers. It was as if he could sense her vulnerable moments, the wretched man.

"Aye," she said. "It feels as if I've been in this saddle for a month."

A slight smile touched his lips, and his gaze swept down to where her legs lay against the saddle. The side pommel turned her towards him, her skirts draped over her legs, and she thought of how he had crawled beneath them at the ball. The touch of his hands and tongue…

Suddenly she was not cold at all. She looked away from him sharply, and to her fury she heard him give a low chuckle—as if he knew what she thought.

"We are almost to Harley Hall," he said. "We're to stop there for the night."

"Hmph. One night to get warm, and back out into the cold tomorrow. Is that kindness or cruelty?"

"To taunt us with a taste of what we can't have?"

Celia looked back at him, startled by the tension in his low voice. But his expression was entirely bland as he looked back at her.

"If it becomes too unbearable, Celia," he said, "you're welcome to ride pillion with me. I would gladly keep you warm."

Celia gave an unladylike snort and stared straight ahead. She couldn't keep the image of his words out of her head—herself perched before John on his saddle, his arms wrapped around her as he rested his chin on her shoulder, his breath warm against her ear.

She thought if she ignored him he would leave, perhaps go and flirt with Lady Allison, who kept giving him sidelong glances. Yet he stayed by Celia's side, riding along in silence for long moments.

"Do you live entirely at Court now?" she finally said, to break the silence and the thoughts in her head.

"Most of the time. Except when my estate requires my attention, which is not very often," he answered. "It is the only life I know. Why do you ask?"

"I have been at Court for many weeks now, and yet you only appeared that day I met with the Queen."

"So you had begun to think you could avoid seeing me again?"

Of course that was what she had thought. But she said nothing.

"Celia, surely you knew we would meet again one day?" he said. "Our world is too small to avoid each other for ever."

"I did think I would never see you again," she said. "I am a country mouse and you—well, after you left so abruptly I did not even know where you went. You could have sailed off to the land of the Chinamen or some such thing."

"I did not *want* to go," he said suddenly, fiercely.

Celia turned to him, startled. His eyes were icy blue as he stared back at her.

"I had no choice," he said.

"And neither did I," Celia answered. She had tried to wait for him, had believed he *would* return. But as days and then weeks had passed, with no word at all, she had seen the truth. He had left her. She was alone.

Suddenly it felt as if a knife's edge had passed along the old scar and it was as raw and painful as when it was fresh. She pressed her free hand against her aching, hollow stomach.

"After you left…after I had to marry…" After her brother and the destruction of her family. "I had to marry Thomas Sutton. His family had wanted an alliance for a long time, though mine was wary of them. But after what happened to my brother I had no choice in who to marry. We had to agree to the union."

"Tell me about your marriage, Celia," John said, and she could still hear that hoarse edge to his voice.

A tense stillness stretched between them.

It was hell. A hell she had only been released from when Sutton died. She had gone on her knees in thanksgiving at her deliverance. But she couldn't say that to John. She was already much too vulnerable to him.

She shrugged. "It was a marriage like any other, but blessedly short."

"Is he the reason you wanted to twist my manhood off when you had it in your hand?"

Celia gave a startled laugh. "I think you yourself would be reason enough for that, John Brandon. And that was not exactly what I wanted to do with it."

He looked at her from the corner of his eye, that half-smile touching his lips as if he too had a few ideas about ways she could make use of him.

"Have you never married, John?" she asked. But did she really want to know the answer? She hated the thought of him uniting his life with another woman.

"You know I have not. I haven't the temperament for it."

"Who does, really? It is merely a state we must endure—unless we are Queen Elizabeth and can make our own choice," Celia said wistfully.

"Yet you will let the Queen arrange a new marriage for you, despite what might have happened in your first?" John sounded almost angry. She could not fathom it—could not fathom him.

Celia shrugged again. "I have no choice. Briony Manor went to Anton, and I have little dower. I will endure."

"Celia…" His hand shot out and he covered her hand with his, holding tight when she tried to pull away. "Tell me what happened with Sutton. The truth."

"I owe you nothing!" she cried. "You have no right to demand anything of me, John. And I will thank you to let me go this instant!"

Her gaze flew to her riding crop, tucked in its loop on her saddle.

"You want to use that on me now, don't you, Celia?" he said roughly.

She jerked against his hand, but he held her fast. It was so infuriatingly easy for him to get her where he wanted her.

"It wouldn't be my hand twisting your balls this time," she whispered.

Lightning flared in his eyes. "I might let you try—if you told me about your husband. About what has happened to you since I saw you last."

The convoy suddenly ground to a stop, and Celia saw to her relief that the gates of Harley Hall, their stop for the evening, were just ahead.

John raised her hand to his lips and kissed the knuckles through the leather of her glove. His mouth was warm on her skin.

"This is not over, Celia," he said against her hand.

Celia pulled away from him at last. "Oh, John. This was over a long time ago…"

Chapter Five

Celia leaned her arms on the crenellated wall of Harley Hall's roof, high above the grand courtyard, and looked out into the night. It was very late—even Darnley and his cronies had stumbled off to bed after draining their generous host's wine stores. The house was silent, but Celia couldn't sleep.

She drew the folds of her long cloak closer around her and tilted back her head to stare up at the stars. They shimmered so brightly in the cold, like diamonds and pearls scattered across black velvet. When she was a child she'd used to lie on her back in the garden and look up at the sky just like this, and imagine she could leap up higher and higher and become part of them. Flying among the stars, letting their sparkle draw her in further and further until she was part of them.

But now she knew there was no escape from the claims of the world. Not among the stars. Not anywhere. There were only the hard, cold choices of the world they lived in. Marriages made for convenience; hearts that had to be protected.

Celia braced her hands hard on the stone wall until she felt the bite of it on her palms. Why couldn't John stay away from her? Why had he ridden next to her today, talking to her, watching her with those eyes as if he waited for something from her?

She had learned long ago that it was much better not to feel at all, to let herself be numb to everything around her. But every time she saw John he chipped away at that ice she'd put around her heart, carefully, relentlessly, until she could feel that terrible heat on her skin again.

She pressed her hands to her face, blocking out the night. Why was he here, suddenly in her life again, reminding her of the fool she had once been?

He had seen the way she'd wanted to reach for her riding crop today, guessed how she longed to lash out at him. To make him hurt as she once had. And that primitive emotion frightened her. It was far too much, too overwhelming.

Just let this journey be over soon, she thought.

Or let John disappear somewhere and cease to torment her.

As if to taunt her, the door to the roof suddenly opened, cracking into her solitude. Her hands dropped from her face and she stiffened.

It could be anyone, of course, but she knew it was not. It was him, John. She could feel it in every inch of her skin, could smell him. Some mischievous demon seemed intent on tormenting her tonight.

She carefully composed her face into its usual cool, calm lines that hid her thoughts, and glanced over her shoulder. She felt no surprise at all to see John there, leaning in the door frame with his arms crossed over his chest as he watched her.

Though the night was cold, he wore no cloak. The crimson velvet doublet he worn at dinner was carelessly unfastened, hanging open over a white shirt that was unlaced halfway down his chest. His hair was tousled, falling over his brow in soft brown waves.

Celia had to turn away from the sight of him before she devoured him with her eyes.

"I should have known you would find me here, John Brandon," she said as she stared out blindly into the night. "You do seem intent on tormenting me."

"I would have said *you* were the one doing the tormenting, Celia," he answered. "Though I would have been here much sooner if I'd known this was where you were hiding. I merely wanted to escape the cursed snoring of the other men in my chamber."

Celia smiled faintly at the disgruntled tone of his voice, glad he could not see it. "And I came here to escape Lady Allison's incessant prattling. The woman has an inordinate store of gossip."

"Then we can be quiet here together," John said.

She heard the soft fall of his boots on the flagstones as he approached the wall.

She stiffened, but he stayed a few feet away from her, leaning his arms on the low wall as she did and looking out into the darkness. Slowly Celia relaxed and listened to the soft rhythm of his breath.

He didn't look at her, but he said, "Your hair is down."

Celia shifted, and self-consciously touched the loose fall of her hair over her shoulder. "I didn't think I would see anyone here. The pins were giving me a headache."

"You confine it too tightly."

"I can hardly parade around with it hanging loose like a girl," she said with a laugh.

"But you don't have to torture it either," he said.

He shifted his body towards her and reached out to lay his fingertips lightly on her hair. He traced a strand all the way down to where it curled under at her elbow. He only touched her hair, but Celia could feel his heat on her collarbone, the soft curve of her breast, the angle of her ribs under her cloak.

She thought again of a predator tormenting its prey, freezing it with the glow of its eyes so it could not flee. Didn't even want to flee.

He slowly wrapped the hair around his wrist, holding her with him. "You have the most beautiful hair I've ever seen. It's like the night itself. I used to dream of it—of touching it, kissing it, wrapping it over my chest as you leant over me…"

Celia gasped at the jolt of heat that went through her at his words, at the flashing memory of how he had once done that. Drawn her hair around him as she'd straddled his hips and bent down to kiss him. A wave of the greatest tenderness swept over her. She tried to pull away, but his hand tightened.

"Tell me about your husband, Celia," he said, his voice soft and yet utterly unyielding.

His voice held her even more than his fingers in her hair.

"He doesn't matter now," she said, fighting to keep her own voice steady. Not to lean into him, wrap her arms around his shoulders. "He is dead."

"For how long?"

"Above a year now. There was a fever that swept through the neighbourhood. My parents died of it as well."

His hand slid up her hair, twisting it around his fingers, caressing it over his skin. His blue eyes glowed down at her in the night, as bright and unyielding as ice. Celia closed her eyes, and she felt his other arm slide around her waist above the cloak. He turned her so her back was against his chest. She wanted so much to give in to him again, not to be alone. To know only him.

"Were *you* not taken ill?" he asked.

Somehow behind her closed eyes, because she could not see him, with his hand soothing against her skin she felt strangely free. Her careful guard slipped just a bit.

"I was ill," she said, a frown fleeting across her brow as she remembered those terrible days. His touch brushed it away before sliding back to her waist. "I had the fever too, though I remember little of it. Only nightmares and that dry, burning heat, a thirst that could never be quenched. I do remember they wanted to cut off my hair, and I drove them away."

"Thank God for that," John muttered, and she thought she felt the press of his lips on her hair. "It would have been a terrible crime to lose this hair."

"I was the only one who caught the fever and lived."

"That is because you are the most stubborn person I have ever known. The devil himself could not drag you down to hell." He sounded so angry, so desperate—just as she felt.

Celia smiled bitterly. "He has tried."

John's hand pressed to her hair. "And when you awoke you found your husband was dead?"

"Aye."

"What did you do?"

To her shock, Celia found herself telling the truth. "I got on my knees in the chapel and thanked God, or the devil, or whoever had done it, for the merciful deliverance."

John's hands suddenly closed on her shoulders and spun her round to face him again. She opened her eyes and looked up to find raw fury on his face, with no polished cloak of civility to hide it. His hands were hard where they held her.

Celia tried to pull back, frightened, but his grasp immediately gentled and his face went blank. He slowly drew her closer, until she was cradled to his chest, and his palms slid over the back of his head to hold her there.

"Why did you marry him?" he asked tightly. "Surely your parents…?"

Celia shook her head fiercely even as she buried her face further into his chest, the soft linen of his shirt. She breathed in deeply of the scent of him, and curled her fingers into the loose fabric.

"I had no choice, and neither did my parents," she said. "After you—left…" She paused to draw a deep breath and her hands tightened into fists against him.

"You surely know what happened to my family then? Everyone knows."

His muscles tightened under her touch and he went very still. "Your brother?"

Aye, her brother. Poor, stupid William, caught up in matters far beyond his understanding. "He was a traitor. Part of a Catholic conspiracy to overthrow the new Queen." That had been the strange part—their family was not religious, beyond attending weekly services at the Protestant church, and her brother had never shown the slightest interest in such things. But he had chosen to go along with his equally foolish friends when they'd conceived a notion to replace Elizabeth with her cousin Mary on the throne, no matter what. And his choices had affected her life too.

"They were obviously quite incompetent at conspiracy," she went on, in the numb, quiet voice that held it all at a distance. "They were caught quite handily and justice was swift. He was dead within a fortnight. And even though my parents retained their estate the fines were crippling. When they died the estate was sold."

"That was why you were married to Sutton?"

Celia nodded against him. "The Suttons had long wanted certain lands from my family to extend their estate. So they got them. But they got me along with them. And an old name to go with their new money."

And she'd got two years of marriage with Thomas Sutton. Her punishment. Even on the eve of her ill-starred wedding she had looked for John, waited for him, prayed he would return. That there was a reason he had suddenly vanished, that he loved her and would come for her. Even after months of silence.

But of course he had not come back, and she had learned that one inexorable truth. She was alone in life. Even now, with his body wrapped around hers, she was alone.

Yet she could not resist one kiss to that bare, warm skin so close. She pressed her lips just over his heart, felt the powerful beat of it, tasted him.

Then she pushed him away and spun round to run for the door. She heard him take a stumbling step after her and she half feared, half hoped he would stop her, pull her back into his arms. But he let her go, and she tripped down the stairs and along the corridor until she found her borrowed chamber.

Lady Allison still slept, and Celia crawled unseen into her narrow bed and drew the blankets over her head. She couldn't stop shivering even as the woollen warmth closed around her.

Chapter Six

John stared ahead of him along the rutted, muddy road, where Celia rode with one of the other men, Lord Knowlton, who had begun to pay her attention. She nodded at something he was saying, a faint smile on her lips, but even from that distance John could see that her eyes were distracted, her fingers stiff on the reins.

Part of him was fiercely satisfied that she paid no attention to the man's flirtations. If she had laughed with Knowlton, let him kiss her hand, John would have had to drag the man from his saddle and hit him in the jaw. He felt as if he walked a sword's edge today, his temper barely in check.

Usually when that darkness came upon him he had to find a brawl or have a bout of rough, hot sex to appease it. Neither was an option today.

He glared at Celia and Lord Knowlton as she laughed at his coaxing words. A real laugh that sounded sharp and rusty, as if she had not laughed in a very long time.

John dug his fist into his thigh, his muscles taut with

the effort not to grab Celia and kiss her until she felt something again—felt *him*. He didn't know if his anger was because she laughed with someone else, or at himself for even caring.

Once he had cared for her far too much. She had slipped behind his defences before he'd even realised, with her black hair and her laughing smiles, her kisses and her passion that burned as hot and fierce as his own. Because of her he had nearly failed in his duty.

And because of what he had done she had been wounded and changed for ever. Every time he looked into her cold, flat eyes and remembered how they had once flashed and danced, every time she pushed him away, that guilt burned in his gut.

And he hated feeling guilty for the scars on someone's soul. Guilt was a burden he could not afford—not in his work. That work had once been his salvation. If he felt the pain of everyone caught in the Queen's justice he would be ruined.

But Celia was not just everyone, anyone. She was Celia. And he still cared far too much for her.

She reached up to rub at her shoulder, a small, unconscious gesture he had seen her make before when she'd thought no one watched. It wasn't a noticeable thing, but he saw her smile slip when she touched herself there.

Now he wanted to pull her from her horse—not to kiss her until she burned as he did, but to strip away her black doublet and see her bare shoulder. Soothe whatever ache she held there. He wanted to take away all her pain and make her life bright again, even as he knew he could not.

"God's teeth," he ground out, his fist tightening.

"Someone is in a foul mood today," Marcus said cheerfully as he drew his horse up next to John's.

"And someone is disgustingly cheerful for no reason," John answered.

"Temper, temper," Marcus said with a laugh. "I'm to meet with Lady Allison's pretty maid tonight. But I'd be happy to oblige you with a fight first, if me beating your pretty face would make you feel better."

"You obviously do not recall what happened the last time we fought."

"I certainly do. My eye was swollen shut for a week," Marcus said. He gave John a considering look. "But that time I was the one in a blind fury."

"I am not in a fury," John said. He glanced again at Celia, who was nodding at something Lord Knowlton said. She no longer rubbed at her shoulder, but she didn't smile either.

"If you say so," Marcus said. "Not that I blame you for being in a temper. A forced journey in the middle of winter could defeat even *my* good mood. And it looks as if the weather is going to get even worse."

John had been so caught up in Celia that he hadn't even noticed the bite of the wind around him, the frost on the muddy ruts of the road that slowed their progress to a crawl. He looked up at the sky to see that the clouds had grown thicker and darker. It was barely past midday, but already the light was being choked off. There was the distinct cold, clean smell of snow on the air.

"God's blood," John cursed. "We'll never make it to the next village by nightfall."

"We'll just have to ride harder, eh?" Marcus said. "At least I have a warm bed waiting at the end…"

The inn was crowded with travellers, all seeking shelter from the freezing rain that pounded down outside, but room was made for an important personage like Lord Darnley and his party. Celia was given a palette in a corner with Lady Allison, and then found herself hastily changed into dry clothes and put in a chair near the fire of the inn's great room for supper.

Celia sipped at a cup of spiced wine as she studied the crowded chamber. Lord Knowlton sat beside her, chatting with her of inconsequential Court gossip as they shared a trencher of beef stew. He had been very attentive on today's journey, staying close to her and entertaining her through the cold, tedious hours. He seemed nice—handsome enough, if older than her, and non-threatening with his kind brown eyes, his polite attentions and compliments.

Usually she stayed as far from men as she could, but she hardly noticed Lord Knowlton when he was right beside her. John Brandon, though—she always seemed keenly aware of where *he* was all the time, even though he had not come near her all day. He seemed to emit some kind of strange, lightning glow that drew her attention to him.

She turned her head slightly to find him again. He sat in a shadowed corner with Lord Marcus and two other men. Marcus had one of the tavern maids on his lap, the two of them laughing, but John didn't seem to see them at all. He stared down into his goblet with a brooding look on his face, as if he was far away from the raucous inn. She well remembered that look.

His fingers slowly tapped at the scarred tabletop, and Celia found her gaze drawn to that slow, rhythmic movement. He had beautiful hands, and long, elegant fingers that were so good at wielding a sword, soothing a fractious horse...

Pleasing a woman.

His stare snapped up from his hand to find her watching him. Some deep, heated anger simmered in those blue depths, and Celia felt her cheeks turn hot.

John had a façade of such elegance and charm, with his fine Court clothes, his handsome looks, his smile. But Celia knew that so much more lurked beneath—a storm of passion and volcanic fury. He could fight like a Southwark street thief—or make love with a force that burned away all else.

She remembered that part of him all too well now, as he watched her across the room, and it made her want to leap up from the table and run. She sensed that part of him was barely tethered tonight.

"...is that not so, Mistress Sutton?" Lord Knowlton asked.

The sound of her name made Celia turn away from John's stare, but she could still feel him studying her. Biding his time, waiting for something from her she couldn't even fathom.

"I beg your pardon, Lord Knowlton?" she said. "I fear I could not hear you."

He smiled, his brown eyes soft as he looked at her. "It *is* rather loud in here. I was merely asking if you planned to remain long at Queen Mary's Court after we have delivered our charge there."

He nodded towards Lord Darnley, who was dicing with his friends by the fire. The man's fine-boned, handsome face was already flushed with drink, his eyes glittering dangerously.

"If he can be safely delivered," she murmured. "It is a long way yet to Edinburgh."

Lord Knowlton laughed. "Hopefully there are enough of us to finish the job. If we can keep from freezing to death in the meantime. Do you look forward to our sojourn at Holyrood, Mistress Sutton?"

Celia laughed, relaxing under the admiration in Lord Knowlton's eyes. When was the last time a man had looked at her like that, in simple admiration that did not twist her up into knots? It was—nice. "I am not sure I look forward to it. Yet I do think it will be interesting."

"To say the least," he said with a smile, pouring her more ale. "They do say Queen Mary is a fascinating lady."

"And a beautiful one."

"Aye, that too. We shall see what her Court is like in comparison to her cousin's. What are you expecting of this sojourn, Mistress Sutton?"

They talked easily together for the rest of the evening, about Scotland and the situation they would find there, about their lives in England, drinking ale as the room became louder around them, the air hotter.

Celia suddenly felt tired. The voices around her were turning chaotic, and she shook her head when Lord Knowlton offered her more to drink.

"I think I should find my bed, Lord Knowlton," she said. "The hour grows late. But I am glad we had this chance to talk together again."

"As am I, Mistress Sutton. Very glad indeed." He raised her hand to his lips, and the look he gave her over their joined fingers was suddenly intense. His mouth opened on her bare skin.

A shiver of disquiet ran over Celia's back, her earlier quiet pleasure in his company dissipating. What had happened to change things? She couldn't fathom what he was thinking about her, and it made her think strangely of her dead husband.

She drew her hand out of his and edged away from him until she could stand up. "Goodnight, Lord Knowlton."

"Goodnight, Mistress Sutton."

Celia turned and hurried away from him, making her way through the crowd. She didn't like the atmosphere in the room now. She only wanted to find her bed and be alone for a time.

But her foot had barely touched the bottom of the staircase leading up to their lodgings when she heard a shout.

She whirled around just in time to see a massively burly man grab Lord Darnley by the front of his doublet and shove him to the wall. Darnley's cronies leaped on the man, tables flew as crockery shattered, and women screamed. The strange tension Celia had sensed snapped into a full-blown fight.

She hurried up the stairs to a point where she could see the fray but not be in danger. Her stomach lurched in fear at the violence, and she pressed her hand to her mouth.

She felt even sicker when she glimpsed John in the swirling melee, a tall figure throwing out his fist to catch a jaw, jabbing his elbow into a midsection, kicking with his booted foot to make a foe go down. There was a terrible grace to his movements, a power, and she wanted to scream his name. To dash into the fray and drag him to safety.

He seized the man who was pounding Darnley's face and threw him backwards. Darnley crawled away, but his attacker bellowed in rage and dived for John instead. John fended him off with a neat sidestep, and ducked under the man's raised arm to drive a fist into his belly.

He didn't see the other man behind him, who lashed out with a splintery log and hit John on his thigh. Blood bloomed on his leg and Celia screamed. Raw, heated emotion and fear overwhelmed her. She raced into the crowd, ducking around the brawlers even as the landlord and his henchmen came to break it up. She reached John just as Marcus did.

"John!" she cried, reaching for his arm as he reeled.

He pushed her away gently, bending to press his hand to the wound. "It is merely a scratch."

"Nonetheless, let's get you out of here," Marcus said, winding his arm around John's shoulders to haul him upright. "Before someone decides to ruin your pretty face. Mistress Sutton, if you would find us a chamber?"

Ignoring John's growled protests, Celia got the landlord's wife to show them to a small room where a fire was lit. Marcus followed her closely.

"Put him down here," Celia said, clearing a pile of mending from the bench by the fire.

Lord Marcus unceremoniously slid John from over his shoulder onto the bench, where John promptly let free a string of colourful curses.

Marcus merely grinned and stepped back. "Whatever she does to you, my friend, you deserve it for jumping into a brawl like that."

"I quite agree," Celia said. She knelt on the floor beside the bench, trying to ignore the hot, angry glare of his eyes as he watched her. That fear she'd felt for him when she'd seen him hit still hummed through her veins and made her tremble. "Why would you do that to save a looby like Darnley?"

"Because it is my task at the moment," he ground out. "If I had my way I would have left him to what he so richly deserves."

"But why?" Celia said. Slowly, cautiously, as if she feared the wolf might snap and bite, she peeled the torn breeches away from his wounded leg. "Why are you meant to be his protector?"

John hissed between his teeth, and his hands curled over the edge of the bench, but he did not pull away from her touch. "He has to get to Scotland in one piece somehow."

"I don't know why," Celia murmured. She delicately examined the bleeding gash on his leg while studiously *not* looking at the smooth, warm skin, the masculine roughness of the dark hair that curled there. "I think it would be no terrible loss if someone *did* remove him from the situation."

John and Marcus looked at each other over her head. "Unfortunately that is not our decision to make," Marcus said lightly.

"Not yet," John added.

Celia didn't really want to know what they meant by that. She didn't want to be involved in these secret matters of crown and families at all. She had enough to worry about on her own.

Such as ignoring what happened to her when she was close to John.

She almost sighed aloud in relief when a maidservant delivered her valise. Celia opened it and dug through the contents for the herbal salves and tinctures she had packed.

As she laid them out on the floor, Marcus said, "I will leave you to your task then, Mistress Sutton. I should make sure all is well out there now."

He bowed to her and turned on his heel to go, the door clicking shut behind him. For an instant Celia could hear sounds from the public room, cries and quarrels and the landlady demanding payment for the destruction. Then she was closed in firelight and flickering shadows, alone with John.

She bit her lip, trying to press down the nervous trembling inside her, and peeled the cloth back further.

The log had caught him halfway between the knee and the groin, leaving a long cut. The bleeding had mostly stopped, was clotting around the edges. She could smell the coppery tang of it, but blood no longer had the power to make her swoon. She had seen too much of it.

But the smell of John—that made her feel light-headed. Leather and wine, the faint whiff of spicy soap, the darkness of his skin and sweat. The musk of his manhood. It was heady, alluring. It made all the old memories of a time when they had been as close as two people could be return to her, so strong.

Celia sat back on her heels, away from the too vulnerable position of kneeling between his thighs, and reached into her valise for a clean rag. She soaked it with lavender water.

"There are splinters caught in the wound," she said. "I have to clean it before it can be bandaged."

His fists curled even tighter into the edge of the bench, and she saw the knuckles were bruised. He had certainly left his opponents in worse shape than he was. But it could have been so much worse. If the log had caught him higher…

"You're fortunate the wound is where it is," she said. She set her jaw in a determined line and leaned forward to dab at the raw edges of it with her cloth. His thigh tensed, but he said nothing. "A bit higher and all the Court ladies would be in mourning."

He laughed. "And would *you* have been disappointed, Celia?"

"Certainly not," she snapped. "I would have sung a hosanna—womankind safe again."

"I don't believe you."

He uncurled one hand from the bench and reached out. She felt his soft touch on a strand of hair that had fallen free in the tussle. He ran a caressing touch down its length.

Celia ground her jaw tighter, determined not to jerk away. Not to show how his touch made her so damnably weak. Made her remember things she should forget—like how she had once cared for him so very much.

"I'm sure you remember how many other delightful things there are to do," he whispered. "With hands and tongues…"

Celia pressed the cloth hard to his wound and he straightened up with a hiss. His hand fell from her hair.

"I need to finish this," she said quietly. "Unless you want it to fester until you lose the leg—among other things."

He chuckled and leaned back as he placed his palms flat behind him. "Do your worst, then, Celia. But I know you do remember."

He said nothing more as she finished cleaning and binding the wound. She tied off the ends of the bandage and sat back on her heels to look up at him.

A half-smile lingered on his lips as he watched her, his eyes dark, his skin gilded a molten gold in the firelight. His doublet hung open, his shirt half unlaced to reveal a chest damp with the sweat of the fight. He looked lazy, considering—like some Eastern king watching a slave who had been delivered to his feet.

Celia suddenly wanted to shatter his laziness, that look of casual possessiveness. She gave him a smile, and his own faded.

Slowly, deliberately, she leaned forward and rested her hand on his unwounded thigh. His whole body grew taut and wary. Celia held onto him and placed her parted lips on the skin left bare by the torn breeches. She moved her mouth over him, tasting him.

"Celia…" he said hoarsely.

She pressed her hand tighter on his leg and he went still. She closed her eyes and kissed her way higher, over the velvet fabric that lay tight over his upper thigh, until she could trail the tip of her tongue along the crease between leg and groin.

She could smell him there, the faint scent of sweat and musk she had once known meant he wanted her. He had left her, but he still wanted *this*, and the knowledge gave her a sudden surge of satisfaction. Of pleasure. At least she still had that. And now she wanted more, wanted to know all of him.

Her feelings surged inside her, so tangled and confused.

Her hand slid up his leg to just beneath his codpiece, cradling him in her fingers. He was already hard, but he grew even harder, longer. She found the vein on his underside beneath the cloth and slid her fingertips along it.

"Oh, aye," she whispered. "I remember all the things one can do with hands and mouths…"

She'd just barely touched her lips to the tip of him when she felt his fingers dive into her hair, tumbling the few pins that were left there free. He pulled her head back until she stared up into his eyes.

Those burning eyes that pierced right through her tore her careful defences down one by one and destroyed them until they were ashes around her.

"Celia, you drive me mad," he growled. Then his mouth drove down onto hers.

His tongue plunged inside, tasting her, claiming her—every part of her. She tried to draw back but he held her fast, his hand tight in her hair, his mouth sealed over hers.

She moaned and tried to push his tongue out with hers, but instead she found it twisting with his, tasting him return. He tasted dark and sweet, like wine and the night and John, and she wanted it. She wanted it with such raw longing it terrified her. She couldn't think, couldn't reason. He was all around her, all she knew.

His other arm came around her shoulders and drew her up until she sat on his lap, balanced on his un-wounded thigh. He never broke the desperate rhythm of the kiss, only drove deeper into her.

She wrapped her hands around his neck and felt the soft hair at his nape brush over her fingers. She caressed him there, trying to learn the feel of his skin, the essence of him, all over again. John groaned, and untangled his hand from her hair to touch the base of her throat, pressing over her pulse.

He brushed aside the edges of her surcoat and traced his fingertips over the bare swell of her breasts above her bodice. His fingers were rough on that soft skin, and she wanted more. She arched her back with a soft moan into his mouth and his palm flattened over her breast.

One finger slid beneath the brocade and swept over her aching nipple once, twice, then harder, making her cry out. His thumb slid in with the finger and he pinched her between them.

Pleasure shot through her, and Celia accidentally fell

back on his lap. She kicked his wounded leg with her slipping foot and he gasped.

"Oh, hell!" she cried, tearing her mouth away from his. She pushed out of his arms and leaped to her feet.

He reached out for her, but she could see the fresh blood spotting his bandage.

It brought her coldly to her senses as nothing else could. He had held her captive in their own hidden world where there were only the senses, the way he made her feel. She couldn't stay there, no matter how much she wanted to. It had already destroyed her once.

"I—I will send someone in to finish tending to your wound," she stammered. John reached out for her, but she shook her head and spun round to run out of the room. She was always fleeing from him, from whatever terrible power lay between them, but it seemed it was all she could do.

Clutching her surcoat closed, she dashed through the near-empty great room and up the stairs. Past the sleeping bodies to the palette where Lady Allison already slumbered.

Trembling, Celia shed her clothes as best as she could and slid under the blankets in her chemise. She closed her eyes tightly, trying to find sleep, to forget John Brandon, even as her body still felt tingling with newly aroused life.

"Why, Mistress Sutton," she heard Lady Allison whisper, "you naughty thing."

Celia's eyes flew open and she peered at Allison over her shoulder. Allison grinned at her, as if they were conspirators.

"Is he as wonderfully skilled as they say?" Allison whispered.

Celia felt her cheeks grow warm. Ashamed of that ridiculous blush, she turned away and closed her eyes again as Lady Allison softly laughed.

Oh, aye, she thought bitterly. John Brandon was entirely too skilled for any woman's good.

Chapter Seven

John shifted in his saddle, trying not to wince as his bandaged leg brushed the hard leather. It had been some time since he had indulged in a tavern brawl, despite his reputation for wildness, and he felt every bit of the violence in his bruised muscles and the healing gash on his leg.

But it was worth every ache just to remember how Celia had cared for him, bandaging his wound, kneeling between his knees. Kissing him so passionately, so wildly, as if he was all that mattered to her.

Just as he had felt when his lips touched her, tasted her. Nothing else existed. Nothing had ever come between them.

That had been last night. Everything was always different in the cold light of day.

And a damnably cold day it was. Snow had set in soon after their hasty midday meal of bread and cheese—great fat flakes that melted on his cloak and drifted into white piles at the side of the road. The wind felt like needles as it swept around them. Even Lord Darnley, his pretty face bruised and sulky after last night, has subsided into the silence of endurance.

John looked to where Celia rode in one of the carts, lodged between the meagre shelter of two travel trunks. The hood of her black cloak was drawn over her hair, and he could see only the curve of one pale cheek. The long, thick lashes that cast shadows over her cheekbone as she stared down at the book in her gloved hands.

She hadn't turned a page in fully fifteen minutes. John knew because he had been watching her the whole time. Yet she was not asleep. Her shoulders and slim back were too stiff and straight.

She never looked his way, never indicated by the slightest gesture that she knew he was there. Her walls were back up, her drawbridge slammed closed to him. It would be best for both of them if he just let it stay closed. Old scars did not need to be ripped open all over again.

Yet still that desire burned deep inside him to see her eyes free of that caution, that icy chill, to see *his* Celia again. To make her admit she had never ceased to be his.

But she was *not* his. She never had been. It had all been a terrible mistake. He couldn't let her touch his heart as she once had—until he'd found out her brother was one of the conspirators he had come to the countryside to catch. Too late, for by then he had already fallen for Celia.

"You look as if last night's fight was merely a prelude to what you'd like to do today," he heard Marcus say as his friend's horse fell into step beside him. "You look furious."

"Then shouldn't you best stay away from me?" John growled.

"I'm not that easily frightened," Marcus answered carelessly. "If you need to beat on someone that badly, Darnley is over there. But I don't think that would help."

"Of course it wouldn't. The Queen would have my hide if I damaged her pretty pawn."

"I mean I don't think violence will ease you. When were you last with a woman?"

John slanted a hard warning look at his friend. "Marcus…"

"That long, eh? No wonder you're so fierce."

Aye, John thought, it had been a while since he tupped a woman. Since before he'd seen Celia again. Now it seemed when he looked at another woman, talked to her, saw her smile of invitation, it stirred nothing at all within him. It was not enough.

"Lady Allison is always up for a lark, you know," Marcus said, as if heedless of the turmoil within John. "Or Mistress Andrews. She is meant to be Darnley's *inamorata* right now, but she's bound to be bored waiting around for him to get it up. Or the next town is sure to have a decent brothel—"

"I don't need you to play pimp for me, Marcus," John interrupted.

"Of course you don't. Women fall at your feet everywhere you go. You hardly have to seek them out. But you need *something* to free you from whatever demon has you in its clutches."

John grimly shook his head. "Just leave, Marcus."

"So you can go on brooding? Nay, we have been friends for too long. I know this journey is hellish, but there is something more. What is it?" Marcus's tone had become suddenly serious. He and John had known each other for too long—through their wild youths and into this dangerous work.

John's stare unconsciously went to Celia, where she sat in the cart. Lord Knowlton was with her now, and she smiled at whatever he'd said to her, just as she had when the man had sat with her in the tavern last night. She seemed to like him too much.

His hands tightened into fists on the reins.

"Ah," Marcus said softly. "I see."

John tore his eyes away from Celia to glare at Marcus. "What do you see?"

"Every time the two of you are together I would vow you are about to murder each other or strip each other's clothes off—or both."

A wave of despair rolled over John, hard and cold. All his years of careful subterfuge and one moment with Celia pulled all the lies and façades away. He was being such a fool. "Am I so obvious?"

"Only to me, as I would be to you. To everyone else you are still the rakish, careless Sir John Brandon. But I have never seen you like this with a woman. What is she to you?"

John glanced around to see that they had fallen slightly behind the others and no one was near. They were all too occupied in their own cold misery to pay attention to anyone else.

"A few years ago, when I was in the country on a task, we had a—dalliance," he said.

Marcus gave a low whistle. "And I take it matters did not end well?"

Considering he had betrayed her brother and his friends to their death, nay, it had not ended well, and he had left Celia—and his heart—behind. And he had never forgotten her since. "Nay," he said shortly.

"But you still want the lady?"

John said nothing, and finally Marcus laughed. "Then I think we can look forward to many more brawls on this journey. Unless you make love to Mistress Sutton again, get past those icy walls of hers and rid her from your system."

"Do you really think she would let me in her bed again, knowing all she does now?" John said bitterly.

Marcus said nothing in reply, and they rode on in heavy silence.

"Halt!"

Celia glanced up from the book she held in her hands to see the head of Lord Darnley's guard blocking the procession on the road. She had not been reading at all, merely staring at the book as she felt John stare at her. As last night's kiss flashed through her mind over and over.

Something had shifted between them in that kiss, something she sensed was profound even as she could not decipher what it was. What a hold on her he still had.

She was glad of any distraction. She put the book back in her saddlebag and slid off the cart, holding onto the wooden slats as the legs she had tucked under her cramped. Everyone else had come to a halt as well, looking relieved to stop. The day had only grown more bitterly cold, the snow falling thickly.

"The bridge across the river ahead is out," the guard said. "We can either turn back and make camp, or go downstream to the next bridge and continue to the next manor."

Either way, they were surely in for more cold. Celia sagged back against the cart as she watched the guards consult with Darnley and his men. It looked as if they would be here for a time. Celia turned and made her way through the milling crowd, away from the noise, until she found a silent spot on the sloped icy banks of the river. She wrapped her arms around herself and stood there very still, watching the freezing water rush past below her.

Surely this journey would never end? She would never be free of John, of seeing him every day and re-membering. Remembering the foolish girl she had once been, how much she had wanted him. How much she *still* wanted him, curse it all.

She heard a soft footfall crunch on the frosty ground behind her, heard a breath, and she knew without turn-ing who it was. She always felt when John was near.

"You seem to enjoy spending time with Lord Knowl-ton," he said roughly.

Celia almost laughed. Was that *jealousy* in his tone? Surely not. That was too ridiculous. He was always sur-rounded by women. "He is charming."

John gave a half-snort, half-laugh. "Of course he is. He wants to tup you."

"He is a gentleman!" Celia protested, trying to dismiss the feeling of disquiet she had felt with Knowlton.

"So am I," John said solemnly.

Celia shook her head. She turned to look at John and found he wore a fierce scowl on his face, his hands curled into fists. Because she had been talking with Knowlton? He had no right to care. Should *not* care. And she should not be feeling as she did either. As if her whole being was wound so tightly she might burst.

"John, you are the very furthest thing from a gentleman there could be," she said.

"God's teeth, Celia, don't push me away like this any more!" he suddenly shouted.

He moved so fast she couldn't back away, lunging forward to seize her arm and pull her towards him.

"Tell me what you're feeling. Tell me how I make you feel."

How he made her feel? Anger and pain as she had never known, everything she had locked inside her for so long, rose up in her like the fiery force of a volcano. It exploded from her, and she lunged forward to slap John across the face. "You left me!" she cried, all the pain of years ago flooding out of her. "Tell me why you did that? Tell me how you felt then. Tell me…" She slapped out at him again as he instinctively stepped back.

In her blindness, she caught him low on the jaw with the flat of her hand. It wasn't a hard blow, but he was caught by surprise and fell back a step. She reached out to hit him again, and he caught her wrist in his hand.

His fingers tightened on the slender bones there and she sobbed as she struggled to break free.

The flash of fury in his eyes, of some pain that answered her own, made her sob again.

"You have no right to question me, John Brandon," she cried raggedly. "You have no right to say anything to me at all. You left me. You have no part in my life!"

"Celia…" he began, his voice tight as if he too was on the brink of an explosion. As if he held himself tightly leashed.

"Nay! I survive however I can now. And you— you…"

His fingers closed even harder on her wrist, a manacle she couldn't escape from, and he reeled her closer. She tried to dig her boots into the frozen mud, but he was stronger.

His stare was so glittering, so intense. No one had ever looked at her like that before—as if he *knew* her, was part of her. Yet he wasn't. Hadn't been in so long. She had been alone.

She wanted only to leave him, to run and hide, to be free at last of whatever hold he had on her. She twisted her body hard as it touched his, trying to wrench away. But she overbalanced on her uncertain feet and fell heavily to the side.

Her hand was pulled from John's at last, yet she couldn't right herself. She felt herself toppling to the ground.

"Celia!" she heard him shout.

As she fell heavily onto the ice her leg caught on a fallen branch and she rolled forward. She had only a dizzy glimpse of him, of the raw horror on his face, of the flat grey sky above her, and then she was tumbling down the steep riverbank. Faster and faster.

She tried to catch at the ground, at anything she could find, but it slid out of her grasp. Her head struck something and bright stars whirled around her. Her whole body seemed to go numb.

Yet she felt it when she tumbled into the water. The icy-cold waves closed over her head, and it felt like a thousand daggers plunging into her skin. She tried to scream at the agony, and water rushed into her mouth.

Celia did know how to swim, and she struggled to push past the pain and fight her way to the surface. Her heavy skirts and boots grew sodden, weighing her down. She kicked hard against them and managed to break upwards and gulp in a precious breath. But the river wasn't finished with her yet. It caught at her again, pulling her down.

And suddenly she only wanted to *live*. When her brother had died, when she'd been with Thomas, she had never really wanted to die. But merely surviving, putting one day behind her and then the next, had been all she could do. Otherwise the pain and anger would overwhelm her.

But now, with her whole body numb and the rushing river carrying her away, she wanted life again. Music and colour and sunshine. She wanted to see John—to slap him properly, to find out once and for all what had really happened when he left her. Or to kiss him as she once had, with nothing held back.

That was her last thought as she was sucked under the water again. The precious air was cut off.

Suddenly a hard arm caught her around her waist and jerked her up towards the light.

She gasped and let her head fall back onto a naked shoulder as she was drawn towards the shore. It seemed so very far away, yet she wasn't scared now. Somehow she knew it was John who held her, and that he wouldn't let her go. He wouldn't let the river have her.

He reached the bank and hauled her up its slippery length under his arm. Celia couldn't stop shivering, couldn't think. When they reached the top, he laid her on the ground and pulled up her skirt, to draw her own dagger from its sheath at her thigh.

He cut away her sodden doublet and the stays beneath in smooth, quick strokes and spun her onto her stomach, his legs straddling her hips. The flat of his hand hit her hard between the shoulderblades once, twice, until she expelled the water that choked her lungs.

She sobbed out all her fear and relief, and through her tears she felt him pull her back into his arms. He wrapped his body all around her, all his heat and strength. He pressed his lips hard to her cheek, and to her shock she felt his own tears on her skin.

"God's teeth, Celia," he growled. "I thought you were dead. I thought…"

"You saved me," she sobbed through her chattering teeth. "You—you could have drowned."

"I won't let you go," he said. "Not without me."

Celia heard a shot and the pounding of running feet on the icy mud.

"John!" Lord Marcus said, and for once there was no lightness at all in his voice. "What happened? Are you hurt?"

"She fell into the river," John answered. He still held onto her.

"Oh, sweet God, Mistress Sutton, but you will surely freeze to death!" Lady Allison cried.

Celia heard the swish of fabric and a warm, fur-lined cloak covered her icy skin.

She was drawn away from John even as she tried to hold onto him. "Nay," she cried.

But darkness closed in on her, born of the cold and shock, and she fainted into its weighty oblivion.

Chapter Eight

"Shh. Be still. Rest now." John slowly smoothed the cool, damp cloth over Celia's brow and whispered to her until she settled back in the bed. She still frowned, and her hands were curled tightly against the sheets as if she fought demons in her sleep. But she quieted.

John sat back in his chair by the bed and ran the cloth over her shoulders and along her arms. It had been three days since she'd tumbled into the icy river—three days that they'd been alone in the small hunting lodge tucked into the woods. The chills and fever that had come upon her seemed to be subsiding, but sometimes he feared that was his own wishful thinking. His own fear of losing her all over again—for ever this time.

He balanced her hand on his palm and studied the delicate pale fingers. She had survived the fever that killed her parents and husband because her delicacy hid a fierce spirit. He had told her she was the most stubborn person he had ever seen, and she was. She would survive this. He would make certain of it. He would use all his strength to pull her back to him.

Once he had dared to begin to think of a future with someone else, with Celia. Could he afford to think of that now? What could he offer her? She was in this place now because of him. He never wanted to hurt her again.

"I should never have quarrelled with you that day, Celia," he whispered. He should have known she would fight like the warrior she was, his fairy queen with claws. But he wasn't willing to let her hurt herself.

He laid her hand back on the sheets at her side and went on bathing her skin. She felt cooler to his touch now. Most of the heat on her bare arms was from the fire he had built up in the grate. She wore a chemise with the sleeves cut away, a bandage wrapped above the elbow, where the physic had bled her before the others moved on with their journey. Her hair fell over one shoulder in an untidy black braid.

John slowly smoothed the cloth up her arm and over her collarbone. He saw again the shoulder that had had him so furious when he first undressed her.

It had obviously been damaged, wrenched out of its socket and then reset improperly, so that it stood out crookedly under her smooth white skin. Pale scar tissue lay in a pattern over it. There were also faint marks on her back and buttocks, thin white scars that had not been there when they'd made love three years ago.

Her bitterness and distance, her hatred of her husband and gratitude for his death, made terrible sense now. If the man hadn't already been dead John would have killed him with his own hands, in a slow, terrible way involving red-hot pokers and dull daggers.

But torturing Thomas Sutton wouldn't bring his Celia back. How could he do that?

"You have to fight to live now, my fairy queen," he said fiercely. "Fight so you can go on hating me." Go on punishing him. He deserved no less. Yet he could never bear it if Celia died. She would take with her every dream he'd ever had of a better life than the one he led.

"Fight, damn you!" he shouted.

"Oh, John, do leave me alone," she murmured hoarsely. "I cannot sleep with so much noise."

John's eyes shot to her face. Her eyes were open and clear, not glassy from the fever, and she watched him as if she actually saw him, not some nightmare hallucination.

"Celia, you're awake!" he said, and a new happiness pushed away the fear and fierceness. He carefully took her hand in his, reassured when her fingers weakly squeezed his.

"Am I?" she said. She carefully shifted on the bed, frowning. "I feel as if I've been drawn and quartered. Where are we?"

"At one of the Queen's hunting boxes. Luckily one of Darnley's cohorts remembered it was nearby."

"Nearby what?" She looked terribly confused, so young and vulnerable.

"Do you not remember?" John asked.

"I remember riding in the cold. It was snowing…" Her eyes widened. "I fell into the water! I wanted you to tell me…something."

John shook his head. "And you caught a feverish chill. We've been here three days."

"Three days?" Her gaze darted quickly around the chamber: the large bed, the faded tapestries on the walls, the fire. The freezing rain that lashed at the mullioned window. "Alone?"

"Don't worry, Celia," John said with a teasing grin. He suddenly wanted to burst out laughing like a fool, to shout with exultation. She was awake! He could face anything if she would only stay alive, stay with him. "I am not in the habit of ravishing unconscious females."

"But you came in after me. How are you not ill?"

"I was not in the water as long as you. And we can't both be ill."

She glanced down at her body under the sheet, at the bandage and the basin of cool water. "You have been taking care of me?"

"The others had to continue on their journey if they were to make it to Holyrood when expected. And that cursed Darnley was fearful of contagion."

"It would serve him right," Celia muttered. She shifted on the bed. "I'm so thirsty."

"Here, take some wine. The doctor said it would strengthen your blood, but you haven't been able to keep it down." John slid onto the mattress beside her and eased his arm around her shoulder to help her sit up against his shoulder. She shivered, and he frowned as he felt how thin she was under the chemise.

Celia was too slender anyway, much thinner than she'd been three years ago. Until they were able to travel and catch up to the others John would see to it that she ate, that she grew strong again. A heated, tender rush flowed over him as he looked at her.

He held up a goblet of fine, rich red wine to her lips and she drank deeply. When it was gone, he eased her back down to the pillows and tucked the blankets around her.

"Could you take some broth?" he asked.

She shook her head. "I feel so tired."

"Then just sleep now. You will feel stronger in the morning."

He started to leave the bed, but her hand reached out to grasp his arm.

"Stay with me?" she whispered.

He looked down into her eyes, now the pale grey of a winter's day. She looked back. Steady, calm. Beseeching.

Oh, how he wanted to stay with her. To hold her close in his arms and feel her breath, her heartbeat, the very life of her. Even as he knew he should stay away from her, not hurt her any more, he couldn't stay away.

He lay slowly down on the bed beside her and she turned onto her side, her back to his chest. John wrapped his arms around her waist and felt her relax with a sigh. She was with him now, in this moment. That was all that mattered for now. All that had ever really mattered.

"Thank you," she breathed, and sank down into healing sleep.

But John stayed awake all night, cradling her against him and remembering all he had lost when he'd lost her. Did he dare hope to get it back?

* * *

Celia slowly drifted up from her soft, dark sleep, becoming aware of the world around her again. It had been a good sleep, not the plague of nightmares like before, and her body didn't ache and burn. She could feel a soft pillow under her cheek, clean linen sheets around her shoulders, the brush of a fire's warmth on her face.

Everything felt so quiet and peaceful. Safe. When had she ever felt safe? She couldn't even remember. Had she died and gone to heaven, then? She slid deeper into the warm cocoon of the bedclothes—and then she truly remembered where she was. Who was with her.

John. He had pulled her from the river, had nursed her here, just the two of them alone. It felt so strange to be here with him, it felt—right. Yet she had been so angry with him. She was utterly confused.

Slowly, carefully, Celia raised her head from the pillow and opened her eyes to look around. She had vague memories of John holding her as she fell asleep, lying on the bed with her. He wasn't there now, she was alone on the wide feather mattress, but she could see the imprint of his head on the pillow beside her.

Holding the sheet against her, she sat up. She realised she wore only a chemise with the sleeves cut away, one arm bandaged. Had she done that? Undressed herself, torn away her sleeves? Nay, it had to have been him. And that meant he had seen her bare shoulder.

Celia rubbed at the bump there and wondered what he'd thought of it. Well, he had his own secrets and she had hers. Nothing could change that, not even the most fervent wishes. She had to remember that, even when she felt so overwhelmed with tenderness for him.

But where was he now?

She eased back the blankets and carefully slid off the edge of the bed. Her legs trembled they were so weak, but she held onto the carved bedpost until the dizziness passed and she could stand. She saw his doublet tossed over a chair, and picked it up to wrap around her shoulders. It smelled of him, of that lemon soap he used, leather and John.

It made her shiver all over again.

She carefully made her way to the window, her bare feet cold on the uncovered wood planks of the floor. The diamond-shaped panes of glass were covered in frost, and she scrubbed away a small spot to peer outside.

Snow still fell, a silent white blanket that covered the ground and iced the trees, obscuring the whole world in cold and silence. They were at a hunting box, John had said, and everyone else had ridden on ahead. How long would they be here together?

She heard the chamber door open, and glanced over her shoulder to see John standing there in his shirtsleeves, a tray in his hands. A frown darkened his face, and he dropped the tray onto the table to stride across the room to her.

Celia instinctively backed away, but the window was behind her and she could only go one step before he was upon her. He caught her up in his arms, holding her high against his chest, and turned towards the bed.

"You foolish woman," he said roughly. "What are you doing out of bed?"

Celia tried to kick, to push him away, yet that damnable weakness still pulled at her limbs. "I'm not ill now! I wanted to see what was outside."

"I can tell you what's out there. Snow and more snow." He deposited her in the middle of the bed and climbed up beside her to hold her there when she tried to scramble away. "You've had a terrible chill, and you'll catch it again wandering about in bare feet."

"Then where are my boots?" she asked, to cover what she really wanted to say. She wanted to demand to know why he had left her three years ago, what he felt now—what he was making her feel. But she dared not.

"Your trunk is here. You can have your boots when I tell you you can. Until then you'll stay right here."

"Villainous bully," Celia muttered. She slumped back on the pillows.

John grinned at her, that mischievous smile that brought out the dimple in his unshaven cheek and made such odd, disturbing things happen inside her. She felt so ridiculously young and vulnerable again.

"You remembered," he said. "If it takes bullying to keep you here until you are completely well, then I'm prepared to do it. Don't make me tie you to the bedpost."

Celia narrowed her eyes as she studied the new, hard light on his face. She couldn't tell if he was joking or not. She had a sudden vision of herself bound to the bedpost, naked, and John kneeling between her legs with that expression of intent determination on his face...

She rolled away from him, her face feeling embarrassingly warm.

"You would not," she whispered.

"Why don't you try me and see, fairy queen?" he said.

When she crossed her arms over her chest, he laughed. He drew her feet onto his lap and started to rub them gently, bringing heat into her frozen toes.

Celia slowly relaxed under his soothing touch. She let herself lean back into the pillows and closed her eyes. His gentle touch moved in slow, soothing circles over her ankles and her calves, tracing a light pattern over her skin that felt delicious.

She knew she should pull away from his touch, hold herself back from him, but she was so tired, so horribly weak. It felt too good to feel his touch, not to be alone just for a moment. To remember all the good things about when they had first met.

"You said we are at a hunting box of the Queen's?" she asked.

"Aye, though not one that's been used since her father's day, I would wager. This is the only chamber that has any furniture. Everything else is covered with dust."

"But there is food?" she said, remembering the tray he brought in.

"They left us provisions. There is broth and bread there, and I'm going to make sure you eat every bite."

"You *are* a terrible bully, Sir John." But she smiled as she said it. She could feel her whole body relaxing under his touch.

"Of course I am. A man has to be to get the best of a minx like you."

Celia rubbed her toes over his thigh, feeling the shift of his powerful muscles under the leather breeches. "Just wait until I have my strength back."

She felt him bend down, and his lips touched the inside of her ankle. The tip of his tongue flicked over the sensitive skin there, then was gone.

"I'm shaking with anticipation of that day, Celia," he said quietly. "But come and have your supper now. Or you will never have that fiery spirit again."

After she had taken as much of the broth as she could, and hastily washed in a basin of warmed water, John tucked her under the blankets again and blew out the candles. Once the chamber was dark, with nothing but the flickering shadows from the fire in the grate, he climbed back onto the bed beside her.

She felt him hesitate, felt the tension of his body, but then he drew her against him again, her back to his chest and his arm light over her hip. His palm flattened on her abdomen, and to her surprise she followed her instinct and traced her fingertips over the bare, hair-roughened skin of his forearm.

He went very still, his body taut against hers, yet he didn't draw away. Celia closed her eyes and just let herself feel him under her fingers, his chest curved around her protectively. The ice pattering at the window, the crackle of the fire, seemed to enclose them in their own little world. Their own special moment. The anger had drained away, and there was only the warm tenderness of old memories she hadn't let herself think about for so long. It was one moment out of real time.

Maybe that feeling of deceptive security was what made her open her mouth and ask, "Where did you go? When you left your uncle's house in the country?"

His hand tightened, and she closed her fingers over

his arm to keep him from moving away. She didn't want to lose the good feelings with him. Not just yet.

"I went to Paris," he said brusquely.

"Paris?" She wasn't quite sure what answer she'd expected, but it hadn't been that. He'd gone to France? So very far away? To get away from her, from their flirtation that had burned so out of control? Was that why he had left so suddenly?

And what had he found in Paris?

"I was given a position in the ambassador's household," he said.

"How long were you there?"

"Above two years," he answered.

Two years—at the most sophisticated, licentious Court in Europe. No wonder he had forgotten his country dalliance. Celia turned her face into the pillow and tried to force away the old pain that was trying so hard to rise up in her again. She didn't want that again. Not yet.

"I was told I had to return to London for a new task," he said. "But I had other work to perform on the journey."

Celia gave a laugh. "Perhaps you would have stayed in France if you'd known the *task* was minding Lord Darnley and the Scottish Queen."

John laughed too, and his warm breath stirred the loose hair at her temple over her skin. It made her shiver despite the warm room, and that tenderness she had always felt towards him returned. So dangerous.

"Perhaps I would have. But then perhaps I would

have returned much sooner if I'd known you were here, Celia."

He brushed aside her hair and kissed her just beside her ear. At the touch of his lips she closed her eyes tightly, and thoughts of French ladies and what John might have done with them flew out of her mind. Only this moment mattered.

John kissed her cheek, and the corner of her mouth. The tip of his tongue touched her, but when she opened her mouth to make him kiss her properly, he drew back.

His arm tightened around her and pulled her closer against his chest. He tucked his legs along hers, their bodies perfectly aligned. She could feel his erection on her backside, but he just pressed his mouth to her ear and whispered to her.

"Sleep now, Celia," he said. "You need your strength. Especially if you still think you can give me that whipping you promised."

Celia laughed and closed her eyes. She *was* tired. Her whole body was sore from fighting off her illness. Yet she feared that when she slept her dreams would be filled with images of John, stripped naked and stretched out on his stomach across the bed as he waited for her pleasure, his blue eyes aglow with tenderness…

John held Celia against him closely as she slept, listening to the soft, even sound of her breath, feeling the movement of her, the wondrous life of her. For a few moments there, in the depths of her fever, he had feared to lose her. He had already lost her once. He wasn't sure he could bear it again—not when death was such a great severing and he'd never been able to make things right for her again.

And all he wanted to do now was make things right for Celia, as he should have done so long ago. If only he knew how.

Celia sighed in her sleep and curled into him, trusting him in her dreams as she could not when awake. He smoothed tendrils of her dark hair back from her brow and thought of the first time he'd seen her. It was a moment he had never been expecting—a moment like something in a sonnet or a madrigal—something he would have scoffed at before he knew Celia.

His youth had been a mostly wasted one, his years at Cambridge a tangle of drink and women and brawls, until one particularly vivid fight had caught his uncle's attention and he'd been forced to find a new direction in his life. Forced to take the chance to redeem himself by serving the Queen. He'd been sent to the country to ferret out the participants in a rumoored Catholic plot to unseat Elizabeth and put Queen Mary on the throne— the sort of plot that came up like weeds every year and had to be chopped down. It had seemed a simple enough task. An easy way to get back in his family's good graces and make a name for himself with Elizabeth.

But then he'd seen Celia standing across the room at a banquet, dressed in a simple white gown and with her hair loose over her shoulders in midnight-coloured waves. It had seemed as if all the light in the chamber gathered only on her, on her shy smile, the pale, serene cast of her face. Everything had gone so still in that moment.

Everything had changed, and he had never forgotten it. He had always liked women—their voices, their laughter, their soft, perfumed bodies. He'd liked them too much to think of settling with only one, but Celia was different. She'd made him imagine a new life, new ways of thinking and being. Until it all had exploded—as he'd known it would from that first moment.

Yet he still couldn't stay away from her. It seemed he never could.

Celia sighed again, and a frown drifted over her brow as if she saw something in her dreams that disturbed her.

"Shh," John whispered, and she settled in his arms. In her sleep she trusted him.

And in that moment, in the silent, cold darkness of the night, enveloped in their own small world of firelight and snow, they were together. He held her safe. He only wanted to make that moment last.

Chapter Nine

When Celia woke again, she could tell it was day by the pale grey light beyond her closed eyes. Yet she didn't quite want to relinquish her dreams. Not yet. She wanted to hold onto that fantasy world, and to those fleeting moments when she and John were not enemies.

She slowly stretched against the rumpled sheets and realised most of the ache was gone. She only felt a new, fresh energy flowing through her, the brush of warm air over her bare arms.

She turned her head on the pillow and opened her eyes to find herself alone on the bed. No snow fell outside the window; there was just that hard grey light.

She pushed herself up against the pillows and saw that John sat by the fire, frowning down at some papers in his hand. A basin and a length of towelling lay on the table beside him, and he looked as if he had just washed. He wore no shirt, and the damp ends of his hair slowly trailed crystal drops of water over his naked shoulders and chest. That light golden skin glowed with the water and the firelight, as if he was an idol in some pagan temple.

She watched avidly as one drop traced a path through the light scattering of brown hair on his chest, arrowing down to the fastening of his leather breeches. For a moment she indulged in the fantasy that it was *her hand* touching him there, teasing him until that ridged abdomen tightened and…

He glanced up and caught her staring. A roguish grin curved his lips, as if he knew exactly what she was thinking. She felt her cheeks turn hot, and she sank back down to the bed so he couldn't see that she blushed like a silly, innocent girl. She remembered so well that old feeling with him.

"So you're awake at last," he said. "Did you sleep well?"

"Aye, thank you," Celia managed to answer. "I feel much recovered."

She heard the papers he held flutter to the table, and the tread of his bare feet on the wood floor as he walked purposefully towards the bed.

She felt his knee press into the mattress and tried to draw the sheet over her head. His fingers curled over the edge of the fabric and pulled it away as he knelt over her. She found herself staring up into his glowing blue eyes as he smiled down at her. He seemed in a strangely good mood.

"I'm glad to hear you're feeling better, Celia," he said, still smiling. "Perhaps you're wanting your breakfast now? You looked hungry enough just then."

"I…"

Before she could say anything else, his mouth swooped down over hers. Open, hot, hungry, as if he wanted to devour her. It awakened something deep inside of her, that seed of longing and need that only John had ever created. He had caused such pain and anger in her life, but such wondrous things too. Emotions and sensations she had never dreamed could exist.

He still did. And when he kissed her he swept her away on a river of fire.

She opened her lips and drew his tongue in over hers. His taste filled her mouth and she moaned. Oh, yes— she did remember this, so very well. And it made her feel just as it once had.

John's arms came hard around her and dragged her closer to his naked chest. As they kissed, deeper, hungrier, their tongues entwining, thrusting, she laid her hands flat on his shoulders and felt the damp heat of him against her palms. John groaned deep in his throat, his hands fisting in the cloth of her chemise as if he would rip it from her.

Emboldened, Celia slid her caress lower, slowly, savouring the way he felt against her. He was just as she remembered—just as he was in her fevered dreams of the past—only even better. Stronger, harder, hotter. *This* was what she needed. This was what would close her past with him, let her put it all aside. To have him as he was now, as she was now, and know that was all there was. Free of the past, with only the feelings of this one moment to think of.

She traced her fingertips over his flat nipples and felt them pebble under her touch. She scraped the edge of her thumbnail over one and he growled. She pressed slightly harder, hard enough to give just the slightest edge of pain, but he didn't shove her away or slap her as her husband would have. His skin rippled, but he went on kissing her.

She slid her touch lower, feeling every inch of his torso, every bit of his skin. He felt like hot satin stretched taut over hard muscle, and the light whorls of hair tickled her palms. She dipped the tip of her smallest finger into his navel before she moved even lower to the band of his breeches.

Suddenly her boldness fled. She could feel his erection, rock-hard against her wrist.

"Curse it, Celia, don't stop now," he whispered as his mouth left hers. He pressed hot, open-mouthed kisses to her jaw, the soft curve of her throat. He nibbled at her there, drawing the skin between his teeth to nip lightly at her.

Celia gasped and let her head fall back as her hand convulsed against his waist. Her heart was pounding as if it would burst, and she could feel that his was too as his body pressed closer to hers.

His mouth opened on the pulse that beat at the base of her neck, that vulnerable hollow so sensitive to sensation. He licked at it, swirling the tip of his tongue there before he closed his teeth on it.

"John!" she cried, her head arching back even more until the braid of her hair lashed at his arm. She felt him tug the binding free and her hair fell loose over her shoulders. He didn't raise his head. His open mouth swept over her collarbone, the little hollows just at her shoulders, until he could nip at the soft upper swell of her breast. The edge of his teeth scraped over that skin too, and Celia's fist closed on the band of his breeches until he gave a rough laugh.

"You still like that, then?" he whispered.

"And do *you* still like this?" She moved her hand lower, until she covered the hard bulge behind the leather fabric. She slid her fingers down its length, not as hard as when she'd touched him at the Queen's banquet, but slower, caressing softly until he groaned.

She pressed her thumb to that spot on the underside she knew he liked, that had once driven him to such fierce need. He seemed to grow even harder.

Suddenly he pulled her chemise over her head, tearing her hand from him. She knelt in front of him, her body naked for him as it had not been in so long. For an instant the heat of passion faded and she remembered she was not as she'd been then. She was thinner, her breasts smaller. And there was her shoulder. She wanted him to remember her as she once had been, not as she was now.

She tried to turn away, to draw her hair over that shoulder, but his hands were already on her again. He turned her back into his arms, his head lowering to her breast.

"So beautiful," he muttered. "You are so damnably beautiful, Celia."

And when he looked at her, touched her, she could almost feel beautiful again, as she once had with him. As his mouth closed over her nipple her head fell back and her eyes closed. She felt the soft brush of her hair on her back, and the heat of his lips on her aching breast.

He suckled hard, drawing her deep into his mouth. She bit her lip to keep from crying out at the way it made her feel. Her body, which had felt so frozen and numb for so long, roared back to burning life again.

He covered her other breast with his palm, his fingers spread wide to cradle her, caress her. One fingertip brushed over that engorged nipple and a cry burst free from her lips. She felt him smile against her, just before his teeth bit down lightly and he pinched her other nipple.

She reached desperately between their bodies to unfasten his breeches and push them down over his lean hips. His penis sprang free against her abdomen, rockhard and hot. As she touched it, naked in her hand at last, it jerked and he groaned. His teeth tightened on her nipple before he arched his head back.

Celia looked into his eyes and they were burning and dark, the blue almost swallowed in black lust. She bent to kiss the side of his neck, to bite at him as he had with her. He tasted salty and sweet under her lips, of that night essence that was only John. It was intoxicating, dizzying.

As she kissed him she ran her palm down his manhood to its swollen tip. There was a drop of moisture there, and she caught it on her finger to spread it upward again, slow, steady. *Aye*—she remembered this so very well.

John's hands suddenly closed on her backside, his fingers digging into the soft skin as he dragged her even closer. Her hand dropped away from him and he slowly pressed the tip of his penis against the soft nest of damp curls between her thighs. He moved up and down, lightly teasing at her swollen cleft.

"John..." she whispered against his neck.

"So wet—so hot," he growled. He pulled her flush against his hips, and then suddenly pushed her back to the bed. He came down on top of her, his hips between her spread legs, his lips claiming hers in a wild, desperate kiss.

Celia wrapped her legs around his waist and instinctively arched up into him. He was so large, so strong and—and overwhelming. She was completely surrounded by him, by his heat and power. Suddenly she couldn't breathe.

She tore her lips from his kiss and tilted her head back to try and gulp in a breath. Her hands dug into his shoulders as if she would push him away.

But he seemed to sense something was wrong, that the icy hand of fear was creeping over her, reminding her of the horror that was her marriage bed. His hands slid around her waist, and in one deft twist he lay on his back on the bed and she was on top of him. Her legs lay to either side of his hips as she straddled him.

She stared down at him in dizzy astonishment. The air suddenly seemed clearer around her, the fear dissipating like clouds after a storm. She wasn't held down, overpowered. She was free, yet still tethered to John by the light touch of his hands at her waist, the look in his eyes. He watched her with an almost feral gleam in those eyes, as if he was so hungry he could devour her now in one bite, yet there was tenderness there too, so deep and reassuring. His face was set in taut lines of fierce control.

Yet he made no move. It was as if he knew what she needed now: to be in control of what was happening. Celia swallowed hard. She had never been in this position before, never looked at a man in this way. It was—quite nice.

Very nice indeed, she thought as she braced her palms flat on John's chest. She slid them down, down, a slow, hard glide on his skin. He felt so tense under her touch, as if he waited for her, held himself tightly leashed to let her touch him as she would.

It made her want him even more.

She shook her hair back and smiled down at him. A muscle flexed in his jaw and his eyes never wavered from her. She gently moved his hands from her waist and held them to the bed as she leaned down and laid her open mouth on his chest. His hands jerked but he didn't push her away.

She tasted him with the tip of her tongue, and moved to swirl it lightly over his flat, brown nipple. It hardened under her kiss, and she could hear the harsh hiss of his breath.

She nipped her teeth over the arc of his ribs.

"I always remember this, John," she whispered. "Even when I hated you, when I cursed your name, I would remember this late at night. Your taste. Your smell. The way your skin felt on mine. It was as if I could still taste you on my tongue. You must be a sorcerer, to hold my dreams so enchanted by what you would do to me."

She licked at the indentation along his hip, that enticing masculine line of muscle that dipped towards his manhood. She exhaled a sigh over the base of his penis, and sat up again.

"You're the witch," he ground out as he stared deep into her eyes, not letting her go. "No one has ever made me feel like you did, Celia, from the first moment I saw you."

Celia shook her head. She didn't want to know he had thought of her. Not now. She wanted to remember how it had once been. She only wanted *this*, them together, now.

"Sometimes when I dreamed of you at night, John, I ached so much. I had to do this." She closed her eyes and laid her hand lightly between her breasts. Slowly, slowly, she traced her touch down her body, over her abdomen, until her hand lay over the place that was so wet for him she ached with it all over again. *He* had taught her to do this, and she remembered how the sight of her hand there affected him. How it made him explode.

She slid one fingertip between her folds, and that was all it took.

"Hell, Celia!" he shouted, and his control snapped.

Her eyes flew open as his hands seized her hips. But he did not drag her under him to drive into her. He drew her body up along his until his mouth closed over her womanhood. She knelt over his face as his tongue plunged deep into her.

Celia screamed, and grabbed onto the carved wood

of the bed as his mouth claimed every intimate part of her. His fingers dug hard into her buttocks as he kissed her, licked her, tasted her so deeply. She was no longer in control, but she didn't care. She only wanted his mouth, his hands on her. Claiming her. Making her remember—and forget.

His tongue flicked on that tiny knot high inside her, and she moaned. One of his hands let go of her and slid around her hip, until he could drive one long finger inside of her, just below that talented tongue. He moved it in and out, pressing, sliding, until she cried out wordlessly.

"John," she moaned.

"Let go, my fairy queen," he whispered against her. "I have you with me. You're safe."

And strangely she did feel safe, as she never had before. Another finger slid into her, and she felt pressure building low in her belly. Oh, sweet saints, but she had not felt like this in such a long time! Sex had come to mean only pain and humiliation, but now she remembered what it could be, what it had been—with John. Only John. That heat built and built, expanding inside of her until she couldn't breathe. Her whole body was suffused with golden light.

"Let go!" he said, and his tongue pressed hard to that knot as his fingers curled inside her.

And she did let go. She shattered, that pressure exploding like a bonfire within her. She screamed again, her hands clutching at the bed to keep her from falling into the abyss below.

But John wasn't finished with her. He lifted her trembling body off his mouth and pushed himself up to half-sit against the headboard. He drew her down until she straddled his hips again, her open, wet womanhood spread over the tip of his penis.

"Ride me, Celia," he said hoarsely. "I am yours."

She braced her hands on his slick, sweaty shoulders and tried to focus her pleasure-dazed mind. She stared down at him, at the way his lips glistened with her own essence, the way his eyes were so dark and wild with lust. She could smell herself on him, the scent of the two of them blended, and it made her want him all over again. Need him.

And she wanted him to need her just as much. To remember how they had once been together.

She raised herself slightly, until she felt his swollen tip at her opening, and then she held tightly to his shoulders and slid down. Lower, lower, until he was all the way inside of her, their hips pressed together.

His eyes suddenly went blurry, and his head fell back as his hands closed on her waist.

"Ah, curse it, Celia," he groaned. "You're so tight—so perfect. I can't…"

She raised up again and sank back down, over and over, until she found her rhythm. His hips arched up to meet her. They moved together, harder, faster. Until she felt her climax building up all over again.

Her body fell back and she braced her hands on his thighs as he thrust up into her. She closed her eyes and saw whirling stars in the darkness, blue and green and white, exploding around her until she cried out his name.

"Celia!" he shouted, amid a flood of incoherent curses as his whole body went rigid. She felt him go still inside her, the hot rush of him against her as he too let go and soared free.

She let herself fall to the bed, her legs unable to hold her up any longer. She trembled as she felt a heavy, hot languor steal over her, a boneless exhaustion as she had never known before. The beamed ceiling spun above her as she tried to catch her breath.

John crawled up to collapse beside her. They didn't touch, but she could feel the heat of his sweat-damp body close to hers, could hear the rough rush of his breath.

She rolled her head to look at him. His eyes were closed as he kicked his breeches away, his hair falling damply over his brow. She gently brushed it back, and he caught her hand in his to kiss her palm.

She sighed and closed her eyes, feeling the way he pressed her hand flat to his chest and held her there. She felt the brush of cold air over her heated skin. The fire had died away in the grate, but she didn't care. She was too tired and replete to care about anything but John's hand on hers.

"You still talk filthy in bed, John Brandon," she whispered teasingly. "Where did you learn those words? In Paris?"

He gave a drowsy chuckle. "And you still remember everything that drives me insane. Did you really touch yourself when you thought of me?"

Celia smiled. "A lady must keep her secrets, John," she said. And then she let herself tumble down into a deep, dreamless sleep.

Chapter Ten

A lady must keep her secrets.

John heard Celia's words in his mind as he watched her sleeping in the bed they had shared. Cool grey light moved over her bare skin as she lay on her stomach, her arms around her pillow and her black hair spilling over the rumpled sheets. The coverings were low on her hips, leaving her slender, supple back bare to tempt him.

And, God's teeth, but he was tempted. His muscles were coiled to send him striding across the chamber, to grab the sheets and tear them away until she was naked for him again.

Until she opened for him again, let him in, let him see every part of her, body and soul. Until she cried his name and needed him, as he needed her in that moment.

He braced his fists on the table and let his head drop between his shoulders, shutting out the sight of her. Shutting out the temptation. It had always been that way with Celia, even when they'd first met. She had been in-nocent then, more vulnerable, but there had always been that sharp intelligence behind her cool grey eyes. That edge to her words, that unwillingness to suffer fools.

That desire as she looked at him, that passion that matched his own and drove him higher and hotter.

The memory of her had haunted him for years, until he'd become sure he made her into something she had never really been. An elusive fairy queen who'd never existed except in his mind, his dreams.

But earlier she had shown him she was every bit all he'd once thought her, and so much more. He had never wanted anything or anyone as he wanted her. When she'd taken him inside her, her body over his, her eyes burning with raw need, he had gone mad with it. With *her*. He'd dared to begin to think he *could* make it different at long last.

She had been his again, only his. No rational thought, only feeling—primitive, ferocious feeling.

But now he wished with all his might that she would run from him. Push him away and flee so far they could never see each other again. When they came together it was as elemental as that storm outside, and as lethal. They would destroy each other even as they couldn't stay apart.

Secrets. Aye, she had been so very right about that. So many secrets lay between them. How could he ever make it right?

He opened his eyes and reached out for the papers scattered across the table. Marcus had sent them via messenger while Celia slept yesterday, and they were updates on their travels. It seemed all was not well there, and Marcus needed John to rejoin them soon. Something was amiss among Darnley's cohorts. Something besides drink and fights.

More secrets.

John heard a soft sound from the bed, and looked up to see that Celia was stirring awake. She slowly stretched against the sheets, the fabric easing lower until he could see the vulnerable hollow of her back. Just one of the soft, sweet spots he had so recently kissed. He snapped his too-eager stare up from her bare skin to her face, turned in profile on the pillow.

A smile touched her lips, and she looked so young then. So happy and innocent that he almost went to her. Almost climbed beside her on the bed and kissed her, damning the consequences.

Then she seemed to come fully awake and remember. The smile faded into a small frown and her eyes opened.

Celia rolled onto her back—and caught him staring at her. She gasped and sat up straight on the bed, yanking the sheet up to cover her nakedness. John pushed down the sharp sense of disappointment and gave her a humourless smile.

"Good day to you, Celia," he said.

The tip of her tongue touched her lips—a tiny, nervous gesture that sent a bolt of pure fire straight to his groin. She shook her tangled fall of hair back from her shoulders and lifted her chin in a gesture he had become too familiar with by now. Her armour was closing around her again. He had to decipher how to tear it away.

"So it is true," she said softly.

"You can pretend it was all a dream if you like,"

he answered, keeping his voice cool and calm even as his heart ached. He did not want her to think it was a dream! He wanted her to remember every second, every touch and kiss, as vividly as he did. To want him as he had always wanted her.

"I'm not as good at pretending as I once was," she said, just as calmly.

"Just as you like. You don't have to cower there under the bedclothes. I'm not a starving wolf, set to devour you as soon as you move."

"Nay, the wolf is sated for now. And I do not cower," she snapped. Then softer, as if she spoke to herself, "Not any more."

Her words made him look at her damaged shoulder and think of the fear that had flashed in her eyes when he'd pinned her to the bed. The fear that had only eased when he'd rolled her on top of him. He longed to go to her, to snatch her up in his arms and hold her against him until she knew only him. Only remembered him.

But he had not been able to protect her from her villain of a husband. He had to protect her now.

He made himself stay where he was, his fists braced to the table as he watched her reach for her crumpled chemise on the floor and pull it over her head. He had the briefest glimpse of her bare breasts before she was covered again.

She walked to the table where he stood and reached for the pitcher of ale set there. She didn't look at him as she poured out a gobletful and sipped at it. He tried not to stare hungrily at the soft movement of her throat as she swallowed, at her slender fingers wrapped around the goblet. Tried not to remember what she had done with them.

"What are those?" she asked, gesturing with the goblet at the papers.

"Messages from Marcus," he said, forcing his attention back to the documents. "It seems there is trouble."

Celia gave a little snort of a laugh and took a deep sip of the ale. "Now, why am I not surprised to hear that? Is our presence required?"

"Soon, I think. When you are strong enough to travel. I don't want you to become ill again."

She shrugged and turned away to refill her goblet. "It was only a chill. I am perfectly able to travel. Today, if needs be."

"Celia…" That fierce protectiveness rose up in him again.

"I said I can travel! I want to go," she snapped.

The words she left unspoken hung in the air, and John knew what she meant—she did not want to stay there with him. It was what she should feel, and yet he was angry. He wanted to change her mind.

"I should send for a litter for you," he said, pushing himself back from the table. From her.

"That would take too long, and you know it," she said. "I can ride."

"Nay, Celia."

She spun back to face him, her eyes sparkling. "Do you doubt my strength after earlier this morning?"

He crossed his arms over his chest, his jaw set in a hard line as they stared at each other. The very air seemed to crackle around them.

She turned away first, her shoulders slumped. "Just see to the horses," she said, her voice small and quiet. "I will get dressed."

He did not want to leave her—not like this, with so much still between them. So much that could not be said. But her very stillness held him away. She looked as if she would crack if he touched her. He could bide his time. He had learned patience in the last few years.

"Aye," he said, and strode towards the door. He let it close softly behind him even as every instinct in him urged him to drive his fist into the wall.

Or to grab her, slam his mouth down on hers as he stripped away her chemise and repeated what they had done earlier.

Celia stabbed the pins into her upswept hair as she stared at her reflection in the window. Even in the fractured wavy glass she looked pale and gaunt, ghost-like. Haunted.

She twisted her hair harder, glad of the sting on her scalp as it distracted her and brought her back to her task. She hadn't been herself earlier this morning. Now she had to find herself again.

She glanced over her shoulder at the rumpled empty bed. Earlier, in those tangled sheets, she had been wild and free. Everything she had held so tightly in check for so long had flown free. All because of John. His touch, his kiss—they had always unleashed something in her she didn't understand. And earlier the pleasure of that wildness had been unfathomable.

Now she wanted to scream with the anger and sad-

ness of losing it all over again. When she'd woken up
from delicious dreams and seen the distant, wary look
in his eyes, the cool lack of expression on his face, she'd
longed to fly at him. Slap his face, scratch at his golden
skin until he reacted to her. Showed her something, anything, that told her he had been affected by their lovemaking. That, despite everything, he wanted her still.

She'd managed to hold herself still, to match his distance with a chill of her own. She had become quite
good at hiding her thoughts and emotions. Sometimes
not reacting, keeping herself apart, had been all that
saved her.

And now, in the cold daylight, she saw that he was
right to stay away. Perhaps their swiving had been inevitable—something that still lay between them from
the past. Their bodies still knew each other, no matter
what their minds said.

But it *was* the past. This was the present, and a gulf
wider than the English Channel lay between them.

She finished pinning up her hair and turned from her
reflection to put the final touches to her dress. Some
of her clothes had been left for her, and she put on her
warmest quilted petticoat and wool skirt, a high-necked
black wool and velvet doublet. She wedged her feet into
her riding boots and reached for her hat and gloves. She
was ready to ride into any battle now.

She hurried out of the chamber where so much had
happened and down the stairs, as if she could flee John
and what he had made her feel there at the same time.
But he waited for her in the cold, empty foyer.

He was also dressed to ride, in brown leather and

wool, his hair brushed back from his face. She let her eyes linger on those strands, thinking of how they'd felt as they slid through her fingers, as she'd used them to pull him down to her.

She turned sharply away to jerk on her gloves.

"You still wear mourning," he said, his voice flat.

"I can't afford new Court clothes," she answered. "My black was the last thing I could get from my husband's cheese-paring family. I couldn't let it go to waste. Are we ready to depart, then?"

John frowned as if he wanted to say something else, but he merely nodded. He swung open the door and a blast of cold wind curled around her.

"Let us go, then," he said.

Chapter Eleven

Celia reined in her horse at the crest of the hill to catch her breath after the hard gallop. She tossed a smile over her shoulder at John as he drew up beside her. Her uncertainties of before had been lost in the exhilaration of the ride, the sheer joy of still being alive.

"I do believe I was the victor," she said.

"So you were," he answered with a grin. "This time."

"I will outrun you again, John Brandon. And again and again."

"I wouldn't be so confident if I were you, my lady. Perhaps I allowed you to win out of gallantry."

Celia laughed. "Certainly you did not. The great Sir John, victor in all his endeavours, bested by a woman? You would never want word of that to spread. It would quite ruin your reputation."

"I don't see anyone here to witness my loss, do you? I would say my good name at Court is safe."

Celia glanced around as he gestured with his riding crop at the landscape below. She still smiled as she surveyed the frozen fields, bisected by grey stone walls. It felt good to laugh and tease with John again, to feel at least a bit at ease in his presence.

In the days since they'd left the hunting lodge they had ridden in silence, saying only the little that was necessary as they'd travelled hard over the mostly deserted roads. At night they'd stopped at quiet inns to gulp down a hasty meal and fall into bed—alone. She noticed he always slept at a careful distance from her, close enough to protect her in a strange place, but far enough that there was no contact at all.

He would take her hand to help her from the saddle, would ask her how she fared, make sure she had enough wine or blankets, but that was all.

Celia was happy to be quiet with him, to keep her distance. She thought too much about him as it was. The bare, wintry landscape they passed offered little distraction from memories of what had happened between them in that bed. The feel of his hands on her bare skin, his mouth and tongue on her, his hoarse moans and curses as they rode each other. She saw the look in his eyes as he watched her. It was all still there, vivid and painful—sweet in her mind.

She glanced at him from the corner of her eye. He was absently patting his horse's neck as he surveyed the land around them, a small frown on his lips. He looked as if his own thoughts were a hundred miles away, and against her better judgement she found she desperately wanted to know what they were. What he kept hidden deep inside himself.

But she feared that if she caught a glimpse of John,

the real John, she would have to share the real Celia in return. That she could not do.

"So this is Scotland," she said. "It looks scarcely different from England."

Or rather scarcely different from the England they had seen in the last few days. Harsh, austere, forbidding northern England, so different from the softness of southern England, the noise and commotion of London. The place seemed like a separate world from all she had ever really known. It was silent and grey-green all around.

Yet she liked it. The very harshness seemed beautiful to her, seemed to respond to something hard and cold and wild inside her.

"Aye, this is Scotland," John said. "What do you think of it so far?"

Celia looked around her again and drew in a deep breath. She even liked the air here, clean and diamond-clear, smelling of frost, green, and the faint tang of a peat fire.

"I like it very much," she said. "I like the loneliness of it."

John gave her a strange look, and she thought she saw a flash of surprise in his eyes. "I doubt there will be any time for loneliness once we reach Edinburgh."

"I dare say there won't. If Queen Mary's Court is anything like her cousin's, there won't be a moment of silence."

"They say she is trying to bring elements of her French life to the Scottish Court," John said. "Dancing, cards, masquerades, hunts. I doubt that pleases Knox and his Puritan cohorts. They thought never to see their French Catholic queen again."

That must certainly be true. Surely they'd thought that with Mary in France Scotland was theirs to run as they wanted. The country's religion, alliances and culture in their hands. Until suddenly she'd returned, with her own ways of doing things.

"Has there been trouble?" Celia asked quietly.

"Nothing serious as yet. Mary has proved strangely popular with her subjects since she returned from Paris—except for the men who thought *they* ruled Scotland and dictated its religion and allies. Threats, stones thrown at courtiers' carriages, ugly pamphlets railing against female rulers. But there will be more to come. That seems inevitable."

"Is that what Lord Marcus's message said?"

John shifted in his saddle. "Knox and Queen Elizabeth aren't the only ones who want to control Queen Mary. She still has her French attendants with her, who have their own ideas of what she should do."

"Not to mention the Spanish," Celia murmured. It was so nice to be able to talk to John like this again, to share her ideas and hear his, to know what he thought of their strange situation. "To have a Catholic ally right on Elizabeth's northern border could only be a boon to them. Is the marriage of Queen Mary to Don Carlos still a possibility?"

"A distant one, perhaps, or Mary would have snapped it up by now. She wouldn't dally with the likes of Darnley if she had the Spanish heir."

"And one of these parties is not causing trouble in Edinburgh."

John suddenly gave her a rakish grin. "Celia, where a crown is at stake there is always trouble. We must make more of it for our opponents than they do for us."

Was that how he lived his life, then? Made trouble for others before they could do it to him? Before she could say anything to him, he tugged at his reins and took off down the hill.

"We need to find a place to stop for the night," he called to her, his words caught on the wind.

Celia dashed after him. The cold wind kept them from saying any more as they galloped over the fields and found the road again. The narrow track was muddy and rutted, clotted with fallen branches, but they made good time. Dusk was falling when they finally stopped in front of a pair of gates that stood ajar.

They were of an elaborate design of twisted wrought iron, surmounted by a family crest, but they were being eaten away by rust. Beyond the gates she glimpsed an overgrown trail winding away between towering trees.

John stared up at the crest with an unreadable look on his face.

"Are we stopping here?" Celia asked quietly.

He was silent for a long moment. So long she thought he might not answer. That he had forgotten she was even there.

Finally he said, "Why not? It's growing dark, and it's still a fair ride into the village."

He led his horse through the gap in the gates and Celia followed. As they made their way slowly down

the path she felt as if she had stepped into a troubadour's song of enchanted forests and ghosts. It seemed
even quieter here than on the hill, perfectly silent, as if
even the wind dared not brush through the bare, skeletal trees.

She could see that once this had been a grand park,
laid out for pleasure rides and pretty vistas, but now
it was all a tangle. She glimpsed a half-frozen lake in
the distance, with a pale stone folly crumbling on the
shore. The gathering evening mist only made it more
mysterious.

Celia shivered.

"Are you cold?" John asked. "We will soon be there,
and we can build a fire."

"I'm quite well," she said, even as that chill danced
up her spine again.

They turned at a twist in the path, and Celia saw a
house rise up before them. It was a surprisingly fine
manor of faded red brick and dark wood latticework
that had once been painted. The small windows stared
down, blank and dark.

Above the door was another chipped stone crest.

"How did you know this place was here?" Celia
asked as John swung down from his horse and came
round to help her dismount. "Have you been here before?"

"Nay, but I heard about it as a child," he said. When
he lowered her to her feet he didn't immediately release
her, as he had been doing, but kept his arm around her
waist. He held her with him as he studied the house

with narrowed eyes. "This was my mother's family's house," he said.

"Your mother?" Celia gasped in surprise. Then she remembered John's mother had been Scottish—one of the reasons Queen Elizabeth had given for sending him here. But John had never spoken of her before. "Where are they, then?"

"All dead. They died even before I was born. After my mother was sent to England to serve one of Henry's many queens. Since my parents died when I was six, it is mine now." He kicked at a fallen chunk of brick on the ground. "For all the good it does me."

Celia blinked as she looked up at him. She had seen John angry, cold, passionate, but never like this. So very distant. It made her shiver again, and his arm tightened around her.

"Come, you should be inside," he said.

Celia nodded. She didn't want to go inside. This place seemed haunted in truth. But it was dark now, and there was nowhere else to go.

John pushed the door open with his foot and led her inside.

She had thought the hunting lodge was quiet and desolate, but it was nothing to this place. Everything in the foyer was so still she could hear the wind whistling outside, creeping through the walls. The floor was warped and cracked, the balustrade of the staircase broken. From somewhere up in the ceiling she thought she could hear the rustle of birds.

She rubbed at her arms through her sleeves and followed John into what had once been the great hall.

There was a large fireplace at one end, and a few broken bits of furniture littered on the floor. He found an almost intact stool and set it by the empty fireplace.

"Sit down and rest," he said. "I'll try to make a fire so we can stay somewhat comfortable tonight. We should catch up to the others by tomorrow."

Tomorrow. Their time together was ending so very soon. The reality of their lives, their two separate lives, grew closer with every moment. She should be eager to leave John behind, to move towards the future. Work for Queen Elizabeth; a new marriage. The past gone.

But instead she only felt colder. Hollow inside. She had been closer to John than she had ever been to another person, no matter how deceptive those feelings had been in the end. Yet she craved it again—that warmth she sometimes glimpsed in his eyes.

She had put him out of her life once. Surely she could do it again?

She wrapped her arms around her waist as she watched him use the remnants of the wooden furniture to build a fire. The flames were slow to grow at first, until they grabbed onto the dry, brittle wood and crackled to life. Celia slowly felt herself grow warmer, steadier, calmer. They were here together now. That had to be enough.

Once the fire was well lit, John brought in their saddlebags and made a quick meal of hard biscuits, dried beef and wine. It was full dark outside when quiet fell between them, broken only by the snap of the fire and the wind outside.

Celia saw the way he rolled his head between his

shoulders and rubbed wearily at his neck. Something softened deep inside of her, and before she knew what she was doing she reached out to touch his arm. She couldn't stop herself. His back tightened, and he gave her a wary glance over his shoulder.

"Lean against me for a while," she said softly. "Let me rub your shoulders. You used to like it when I did that after a day's hunting."

For a moment she thought he would refuse. Would stride from the room and leave her alone. But then he leaned against her legs and let his head fall back to her knees, heavy through her skirts.

She sat on the stool while he was on the floor, so her hands floated naturally to his shoulders. His doublet was unfastened, and she eased it down his arms. He wrapped his arms around her calves as she kneaded at his hard shoulder muscles. His skin was warm and smooth through his shirt.

She pressed her thumbs into the tense knots of his back. "This must have been a grand house once," she said as she felt him slowly relax against her.

"My mother always said it was, when she told me stories when I was a child." John's voice sounded deep and distant, as if her touch carried him far away. "There were grand banquets here. Especially at Christmas. Dancing and music, minstrels' tales here by this very fire. Queen Marie of Guise was even invited here one year."

Celia studied the hall around them, seeing it not as it was now but the way it had been. Could be. The floors polished and gleaming, tapestries on the walls, delicacies piled high on silver plates atop carved sideboards. Musicians playing a pavane in the gallery above as the brightly dressed guests danced.

"It's a shame the house isn't ready to receive Queen Marie's daughter, then," Celia said.

"Who knows if my mother's tales were true?" said John as he leaned back into her hands. "This place might have been a ruin for decades before she was born. She just liked to make Scotland sound like a romantic dream. Z'wounds, Celia, but that feels good! I should keep you close to me after tournaments. You would banish any wound with a touch."

Celia smiled, but she didn't want to dwell on how good his words felt. How much she would love to see him ride in a tournament, her favour tied to his lance. "You remember your mother, then?" she said.

"Some things. She had brown hair, and wore a rose-water scent. She liked to sit by my cot at night and tell me tales in her Scots accent. Sometimes I wonder if I merely imagined all that."

"What happened to your parents?"

John gave his head a hard shake, as if to clear it of old dreams. "Like yours, they died of a fever. I was a mere child."

"I'm so sorry," Celia whispered, and smoothed her palm gently over his shoulder. His skin rippled under her touch. She had not known that, like her, he was alone in the world. To be so young a child…

"My uncle was my only family left then, and he was fighting in France," John said coolly, as if he discussed the weather outside. "So I was given to the Court of

Wards. I met Marcus when we were fostered in the same household, and together we made our own family of sorts."

"And you have never seen your mother's home before."

"Nay." He looked up at her with a wry grin. "Not much of a legacy, is it?"

Celia looked around the hall again. "'Tis more than I have. It could be made habitable again."

A frown flickered over his face. "But I am the servant of Queen Elizabeth. I could be no Scotsman."

Silence fell between them, and Celia smoothed her fingertips over the nape of his neck. A strange and most unwelcome tenderness washed over her.

"You must be tired, Celia," John said, drawing away from her touch.

She blinked away the last tendrils of that quiet, yearning dream and watched as he spread out their cloaks and blankets from the saddlebags to make a makeshift bed by the fire.

"Aye," she whispered. She did feel tired, bone-deep weary, and so very cold.

"Then lie down beside me and sleep for a time. Let me keep you warm." John held out his hand to her, but Celia hesitated. A smile touched the corner of his lips. "I vow I will not ravish you tonight, Celia. Just stay with me."

Celia smiled back, and tried to push away a twinge of disappointment at not being ravished again. She took his hand and let him draw her down beside him on the blankets. She lay on her side, facing the fire, and he curled his body around her, his knees tucked behind hers and his arm around her waist. She felt his warm breath on the back of her neck.

She closed her eyes and tried to give in to the exhaustion that tugged at her, but sleep would not come. It felt far too good to be wrapped in John's arms—too safe, too right. It seemed even more intimate than their passionate lovemaking.

She wanted to turn in his arms, kiss his hard, hot mouth and lose herself in his body again. She wanted that mindless lust, that forgetfulness of need.

She understood physical need. She could even somewhat control it, use it.

But the longings of her heart, unleashed by his tenderness, were tearing her apart.

John braced his hands on the cracked windowsill and stared out into the black, frost-tinged night. Celia slept in the room behind him, tossing fitfully in her dreams for a moment before she settled again with a sigh. He wished he could join her in the oblivion of sleep, hold her in his arms and find peace, at least for the night. Celia had once brought him such a peace as he had never known before.

But tonight they were in his family's home, a place he had thought never to see except in his mother's tales, and it made him feel restless in ways he had not expected. He shouldn't have brought Celia here, but there had been little choice. He'd had to find her a place to rest, to take care of her, and this was the nearest house he knew of.

John turned to study the bare, dusty chamber, so full of crooked shadows and the shifting light from the fire. In the night, it looked almost as it might once have been, the cracked plaster and warped floors hidden. The crackle of the flames might have been the ghosts of old laughter.

Once this had been a home, a place for a family. He had never known such a thing, having been orphaned so young and tossed upon the world alone. He had known only that, only looking out for himself, and for a time it had been enough. Until Celia. But the thought that he could have more had been only an illusion in the end. Much like this house in the firelight.

He crossed his arms over his chest and studied Celia where she lay sleeping, still and calm now, her face sculpted by the light. Her arm was flung out, her fingers curled as if she reached out for something elusive.

Nay, he should not have brought her here. She and this house only made him feel things he should not. He couldn't dream of her again. Couldn't hurt her again.

Celia stirred a bit, her hand closing on the blankets. "John," she murmured.

"I am here," he answered. He moved across the room and lay down beside her, even as he knew he should stay away. Something always drew him back to her, some dark force he couldn't understand. He drew her into his arms and she curled against his chest, soft and vulnerable as she so seldom was when awake.

John pressed a soft kiss to her hair and inhaled deeply of her perfume, as if he could memorise the scent and hold it with him always. "I am here," he said again. "Sleep now."

Celia smiled and fell back into her dreams. But John could not follow her. He lay awake until dawn, holding her there in that house of ghosts.

Chapter Twelve

Edinburgh at last.

Celia stretched her aching shoulders as she rode with John through the city gates and along the narrow, winding lanes of the city. She felt as if she had been years and years on this journey, not just weeks. So much had happened since she'd left London. She hardly felt the same person she'd been before.

But now she was here, the journey behind her and an unknown precarious future ahead. Her days alone with John were at an end.

She glanced at him where he rode just ahead of her and to her side, sheltering her from the worst of the crowd. She should be happy that they wouldn't be thrown together any longer. Happy that he could no longer chip away at her defences, remind her of how she had once felt about him, opened herself to him. He could no longer tempt her.

She tore her gaze away from his muscled shoulders and studied the city around her as he led her onward.

After weeks of travelling the winter-silent countryside the sounds and smells of a busy town felt like an assault to the senses. Shouts and cries, laughter, and the rhymes of food sellers bombarded her ears. The mingled scents of smoke from hundreds of chimneys, fried meat pies, chamber pots and too many people in too small a space were raw and pungent.

John suddenly reached back for her horse's bridle and tugged her out of the way as one of those pots had its contents hurled down onto the cobbled street from a window far above. It ran down to the sloped channel down the middle of the street along with all the other rubbish of city life.

Celia looked up from under her hat brim. The streets here seemed even narrower than those of London, the houses packed even closer together. Everything seemed coated in a layer of grey soot and grime, with snow in slushy drifts beneath windows and in the gutter. The rooftops nearly touched above the street, blocking out what little daylight there was.

Celia looked ahead again, and found John watching her. Ever since they had left his family's house he had been quiet, his face wiped clean of any expression. He was calmly efficient, solicitous of her comfort—and cold. For an instant she thought she saw something flicker deep in his eyes, but then it was gone.

"Are you well, Celia?" he asked quietly.

"Of course. I've dodged chamber pots before in my life."

"We'll be to the palace soon."

"Very good. Though I dare say if Whitehall is anything to go by it won't be much cleaner."

A small smile touched his lips before he turned away. "Hopefully it will at least be warmer."

They left the city's most crowded centre streets and climbed higher up the steep lanes to a more open, airy section of the larger houses. She could see the rugged crags that rose up above the town, blank and austere against the cold sky, and the silent grey-green bulk of Arthur's Seat, a long-dormant volcano. It still looked ominous to Celia, as if it just waited to swallow up the whole land again.

At last they came to the arches of a gatehouse and passed through them to the forecourt of Holyrood Palace itself.

Celia recognised it well from the descriptions she had read. Squat and low, it was built of honey-coloured stone around a quadrangle, rising only two storeys in the front and three at the sides.

It looked surprisingly modern and comfortable. Celia had read that the old palace had been damaged by King Henry's campaign of "Rough Wooing" many years ago, when he'd tried to negotiate a marriage between his son and the infant Queen Mary by warfare and invasion. Instead Marie of Guise had sent her daughter to France, to be betrothed to the Dauphin, and fought on until Henry was persuaded to look elsewhere for a match. Holyrood had been rebuilt in a more modern style, with towers, large windows to let in the light, and battlemented parapets.

There were graceful towers to either side of the

entrance, surmounted by the royal arms of Scotland carved over the door. Queen Mary's standards fluttered from the parapets, the arms of Scotland, France and England emblazoned on them.

Celia followed John over the iron drawbridge and along a wide gravelled drive, around a silent fountain towards the palace. She could hear voices floating from a hidden garden somewhere, laughter and music, growls from the menagerie, but she could not see anyone. The rolling lawn to either side of the drive was deserted, and only guards in the Queen's livery could be seen outside the doors and along the towers.

But as they drew to a halt the doors opened and a woman ran down the front steps. Celia recognised Lady Allison's red hair, and stiffened when the woman gave John a brilliant, flirtatious smile.

"Here you are at last!" Allison cried. "Both of you. Marcus said you would probably arrive today and that I should watch for you."

Celia struggled not to frown as John smiled back at Allison. It was nothing to *her* if he flirted with every lady at Queen Mary's Court! That was his reputation in London—why would it be different here?

Because she had seen another part of him at the hunting lodge and in his family's house, when they had both let their façades drop for an instant. She'd seen that he struggled with something dark and hidden in his heart. She longed to know what it was, but at the same time it frightened her. Fascinated her.

Yet this man before her now looked as if he hid nothing more dire than a need for mischief of the sort found amid a royal Court—sex, sport, drink. He still grinned as he swung down from his horse and came round to lift Celia from her saddle. He held onto her for a moment as she swayed on numb legs.

His gloved hands were hard and warm against her waist, and she had to hold herself stiffly rigid to keep from clinging to him. To keep from wrapping her arms around his neck and burying her head in his chest. Begging him to take her away from here and back to the hunting lodge.

Instead she pulled herself out of his touch and stepped back. His smile dimmed, his eyes narrowing as he looked down at her. Then he too stepped away and turned to Lady Allison. He took her outstretched hand and kissed it as she laughed up at him.

Celia twisted her riding crop between her fingers.

"How is everyone here, Allison?" he asked.

Allison giggled. "I'm sure we will be much merrier now that you are here! But Queen Mary is not at Holyrood, I fear. She and most of her courtiers are off on a hunting expedition. Lord Darnley has gone to meet her at Wemyss Castle. They should return within a few days."

"I hope he has not gone unattended," John said darkly.

"Nay, certainly not! He would vanish into the village alehouse and not be found for months," said Allison. "Most of his friends are with him, with Marcus to keep them steady. That's why he left me to look out for you. And now you two must be so tired. Mistress Sutton—if you care to come with me I can show you to your lodgings and send for some food. I know John here can look after himself quite well!"

"Thank you, Lady Allison," Celia murmured. She followed Allison through the doors, forcing herself not to look back at John. To leave him behind.

Allison led Celia into the dim palace and along a narrow corridor. John vanished behind them. The halls were deserted and cold.

"Certain people have been missing you very much," Allison said as they climbed up a winding staircase.

Celia laughed. "I can't imagine who."

Allison shot her a sly smile over her shoulder. "Can you not? Why, Lord Knowlton has been asking after you every day."

"Has he?" Celia asked in surprise. She certainly did remember their conversations, his admiring glances—the way John had been strangely jealous of him. Her stomach gave a nervous twinge.

Allison laughed. "Aye, he has. I'm sure he will be very happy to see you tonight. And I vow he won't be the only one…"

John took a long drink from his goblet of strong ale, closing his eyes as its rough heat slid down his throat. But there was no forgetfulness in the drink tonight. There was nothing but Celia.

He leaned his arms on the stone parapet of the palace tower and stared up into the night sky. The stars were blanketed with thick clouds, and snow had started to fall again, cold and damp. It was late—long past the hour when everyone had stumbled off to find a bed. John had no hope of sleep, so he prowled the battlements.

He thought of Celia, of how she had smiled and laughed with one of the courtiers left at Holyrood over supper. Smiled—when she would not smile at *him* at all now. It had twisted at something deep inside of him, something he had thought long dead, and it had made him angry. Angry and full of a dark longing.

"You do not deserve her smiles," he muttered to himself. He deserved nothing from her. And yet he wanted so much. Dared to hope for so much.

John took another drink of the ale and wiped at his mouth with the back of his hand. All his life he had been alone, had needed nothing and no one. His parents had died when he was so young he could scarce remember them, and he had made his own way since. His work for the Crown had filled a purpose within him, the yearning to do something great for something more important than himself.

Yet always that hollowness had been there, that hole in his heart. Until he'd seen Celia for the very first time, so beautiful with her shining black hair and her smile— the smile she'd turned on *him*. For the first time that emptiness had vanished.

Until he'd lost her.

"Never again," he vowed.

Suddenly a door flew open somewhere below his tower and amber-coloured torchlight spilled out into the night, along with the sound of laughter. John leaned over the wall to see Allison and one of her swains, along with a few others, dash along a pathway as the snow drifted over them.

And behind them was a slender figure wrapped in a black cloak. She paused to glance over her shoulder and her hood fell away, revealing Celia's pale profile. She glanced up and saw him watching her.

For the merest flash of an instant the loud voices faded, the night grew still, and there was only Celia and him. Her lips parted, and John could vow he felt the touch of her mouth on his.

But someone touched her arm and she turned away, the delicate moment shattered. John saw it was the young courtier she'd sat with at supper. Celia smiled at him and let him lead her away.

"God's teeth," John growled, and drained the last of his ale. He would find no rest tonight.

Chapter Thirteen

"The Queen is approaching!"

Celia looked up from the book in her hands as the page's shout echoed down the corridor. Across from her, Lady Allison put down her embroidery with a smile.

"At last," Allison said. "Now we'll have some excitement."

They hurried out of the small sitting room and joined the flood of people rushing towards the doors. Celia heard the blast of trumpets from somewhere up in the ramparts, announcing that Queen Mary was returned at last to Holyrood. The days of waiting were at an end.

Outside in the forecourt snow was falling in earnest—fat, wet white flakes that piled into cold banks along the walls. Even though it was only afternoon, the sky was a dark grey, throwing everything into shadows.

The servants and courtiers lined the steps, watching as the gates swung open. Celia smoothed her hair, tightly pinned under her black cap, and twitched her fur-trimmed surcoat into place over her gown. She felt nervous as she watched those gates slowly move inward. She hated being uncertain about anything, unsure of her control. She knew Queen Elizabeth's Court, but Scotland was very different from London.

As she folded her hands at her waist she thought she felt the sudden heavy heat of someone watching her, the tingle of it at the back of her neck. And she knew, with a terrible certainty, exactly who it was.

She didn't want to look behind her, didn't want to see him. She had been avoiding him ever since they'd met on the battlements, tried to focus on what she had to do here so she could go back to England. But all her efforts couldn't keep him out of her dreams at night.

She dared a glance over her shoulder and saw him standing in the doorway, his arms crossed over his chest as he watched her closely. He wore his Court clothes again, fine velvets in emerald green and black, with emerald buttons and gold embroidery. A pearl drop dangled from his ear, and his light brown hair was brushed back from his face in sleek waves. He almost seemed a stranger after the man she'd become accustomed to on the road. That intimacy and tenderness she had dared imagine with him.

A lady's hand, soft and white, slid over his arm, and John turned away from Celia. She saw it was Lady Allison who touched him, and John bent his head down to her as she whispered in his ear.

Celia spun away from the sight and focused her attention on the riders making their way closer up the drive. She could still hear John's laugh, low and rough, flirtatiously amused, and her fingers twisted tighter together.

No more, she thought fiercely. She couldn't be distracted by John Brandon any longer.

The lead rider bore Queen Mary's standard, and behind him rode a flock of courtiers. When Queen Elizabeth rode out on a hunt she and her people were a blur of bright colours, feathers and jewels, but Queen Mary was still in mourning for her late husband, the French King. He had been dead since 1561, but still everyone wore greys and dark purples, which made them seem part of the wintry sky.

Yet the sombre colours could not conceal the expensive fabrics, the stylish French fashions. In the surroundings of rough Scotland they exuded sophistication and elegance.

Queen Mary rode in their midst on a white palfrey. She wore black and white, glossy satin and soft velvet, a plumed hat set at a rakish angle on her high-piled auburn hair. Celia could tell she was the Queen because she seemed to tower over everyone around her, the tallest woman Celia had ever seen.

The only one in the party even taller was the man who rode beside her, Lord Darnley. He and Mary laughed together as they rode, their horses drawn close.

When everyone came to a halt at the foot of the steps, Darnley leaped from his saddle and lifted the Queen to her feet, spinning her about with a laugh. Mary laughed in return, and didn't move away when he held onto her waist a moment too long.

Very interesting, Celia thought as she watched them.

Had Queen Mary made her decision already, so very easily? Were Don Carlos, Lord Leicester and some unknown French candidate gone from the competition?

What would Queen Elizabeth think of that?

Queen Mary lifted her hem and hurried lightly up the steps, a smile lingering on her lips. Darnley and the others followed her, but she stopped to speak to the major-domo who waited for her.

To Celia's surprise, the Queen's golden-brown eyes turned to *her*, and Mary's smile widened.

"Ah, at last! My dearest cousin's emissary has arrived." She swept over to take Celia's hand in hers and Celia dipped a startled curtsy.

"Y-Your Grace," she murmured.

"We heard of your terrible accident," the Queen went on, still holding Celia's hand. She spoke English perfectly, but the words were touched with a French accent. Her smile turned concerned. "Have you completely recovered, Madame Sutton?"

Celia could see why Queen Mary was so renowned for her great charm, why it was said every man she met was wildly in love with her. She had the gift of focusing every bit of her attention onto whomever she spoke to, as if they were all she cared about.

"I am quite well now, Your Grace, and eager to be of service to you if I can," Celia said.

"And I am so happy you are here! You must tell me every, everything about my cousin Elizabeth and her Court. I do long to meet her myself, but for now I shall be content with your excellent report!" Her warm-sherry eyes swept over the crowd. "And which man is your rescuer? I am eager to meet him as well."

John stepped forward from the group and swept her a low, gallant bow. "Your Grace, I am Sir John Brandon."

Mary laughed—a soft, musical sound. "Ah, yes, we have heard all about *you*, *monsieur*. My ladies will certainly be eager to meet you."

As she allowed John to kiss her gloved hand she gestured with her other hand to the women who clustered behind her. "These are my dearest Marys, who have been with me since we were children. Mary Seton, Mary Livingston, Mary Beaton and Mary Fleming. And this is Lady Helen McKerrigan, who will look after *you*, Madame Sutton, so you can come to know my Court as well as my cousin's."

Queen Mary laughed once more before she went on, "But she will not look after *you*, Sir John. She has a terribly jealous husband, and I will have no fighting among my people."

John gave the Queen an audacious wink. "Thank you for the warning, Your Grace."

"As if you listen to warnings, *monsieur*. I have seen your sort many times before." Queen Mary laughed again, and held out her hand to Darnley, who slid his arm beneath her fingers. "And now I am cold and must rest. I shall talk with you both more at the banquet tonight."

The Queen swept inside, followed by her courtiers. John gave Celia a long glance, but to her relief he too returned to the palace. Lord Knowlton walked past and gave her a bow and a warm smile. Celia remembered what Allison had said about him, that he admired her, and she felt her cheeks warm at the thought.

"Mistress Sutton?" a soft voice said.

Celia turned to see the lady the Queen had introduced as Lady Helen McKerrigan, she with the jealous husband. She was a petite, pretty redhead, dressed in lilac-coloured velvet and a jewel-embroidered white cap—the sort of sophisticated beauty Celia usually mistrusted.

But Helen's smile was friendly and open. "I am Lady Helen McKerrigan. We've all heard the tale of your near-drowning, I fear! I am very glad to see you have recovered."

Celia almost groaned aloud. She was supposed to be quiet and unobtrusive, to observe everyone around her. How could she do that if she was an object of gossip? "I fear I was merely being clumsy. It was no dramatic tale, Lady Helen."

"Nay?" Helen's auburn brow arched. "Not even your rescue by the oh, so handsome Sir John Brandon? All the ladies here are half in love with him already."

"Are *you*?" Celia said, sharper than she intended.

Helen laughed. "Not me. Did you not hear of my jealous husband?" She took Celia's arm and led her back indoors. "Now, let me show you to your new chamber. Queen Mary has ordered you to be moved to a larger one all to yourself. And I want to hear all about your great adventures…"

Queen Mary's great hall was not as large as the one at Whitehall but it was quite as grand, with a coffered ceiling and a parquet floor scattered with sweet-smelling rushes. Elaborately worked tapestries hung on the walls, and silver and gold plates gleamed on the sideboards, a glowing cave of treasure. Small dogs in jewelled collars dashed about and yapped underfoot.

Celia followed Lady Helen through the open doors into the midst of the gathered crowd as everyone found their places at the long tables lining the sides of the narrow room. English and French words mingled in the air, the Scots' accents even heavier next to the musical Parisian cadences. It was easy to tell Queen Mary's French coterie from her native courtiers as well. The Scots were more colourfully dressed, louder, flashier.

Celia had heard that Mary tried to recreate her life in France here as much as she could, with music and dancing, theatricals, intimate card games. But her Scots nobles were too impatient for that, too rough, too set in their own ways after her long absence.

Celia could see evidence of that dichotomy all around her. Did the Queen think her powerful charm could bring them all together, hold her kingdom firm in her grasp?

Perhaps it could at that, Celia thought as she stood with Lady Helen and watched Queen Mary sweep into the hall. She had never seen a woman quite like her before. It was not merely Mary's height and beauty, her elegant clothes and royal bearing. It was something in her smile, in the great confidence that seemed a bone-deep part of her.

Mary had practically been born a queen, taking her throne mere weeks after her birth. Unlike Queen Elizabeth, who had a powerful charisma of her own, she had never had to fight for her place in the world. That certainty showed in her every gesture, her every easy smile. She owned the world around her and it showed.

Celia wondered with a pang what that would feel like. Not to rule a kingdom, but to be sure of one's place, not to have to fight and scrape for every inch. Not to be constantly on guard. Really to belong.

She curtsied as the Queen swept past and studied Mary's tall figure from under her lashes. She had her hand on Darnley's arm again, their heads bent close together as they talked, and Celia saw that even Darnley seemed to be not the same with her. The sulky cruelty was gone from his handsome face, and it made him even better looking. Younger, lighter.

Mary's face glowed as she smiled at him.

"I wonder who would prevail if Queen Mary ever did meet face to face with Queen Elizabeth?" Celia heard someone whisper beside her.

She glanced over to see Lord Knowlton watching her, a half-smile on his face.

"I am not sure," she answered slowly. Lord Knowlton also looked different here in the amber torchlight—older, more serious. Harder. "But I think I would very much like to witness it."

His smile widened. "Queen Mary thinks she could charm even her prickly cousin and they would be amiable neighbours for ever after."

Celia watched the Queen sit down on her dais, Darnley beside her. "I think that might require a bit more than charm."

"A miracle, mayhap?"

Mary gestured for everyone to be seated, and Celia let Lord Knowlton lead her to a place at one of the tables, their shining lengths laid with the finest silver plates and gilded baskets of white bread interspersed with elaborate salt cellars and ewers of wine. Pages rushed past, laden with serving trays of fragrant delicacies.

"I am most happy to see you looking so well again, Mistress Sutton," Lord Knowlton said as he slid a choice morsel of spiced chicken onto her trencher.

"Thank you, Lord Knowlton. I am happy to feel well again." Celia took a sip of her mulled wine and carefully studied the crowd around her, listening to the chorus of their loud voices and laughter, examining their faces.

None of them was John. She didn't see him anywhere in the hall, and slowly she let herself relax and enjoy the fare spread lavishly before them, and Lord Knowlton's conversation. He really was an interesting man, and knew a great deal about music and poetry as well as vast amounts of amusing Court gossip. Which lady had had a romance with which lord, who had come to blows over the Queen's favours, which Frenchman hated which Scot and vice versa. All fascinating and useful.

Celia even found herself laughing at some of his light flirtations. He did not make her emotions boil up inside her as John did, did not make her feel angry and frightened and full of dark desire. He was merely amusing, kind. She could not imagine why once he had disquieted her.

Perhaps Queen Elizabeth would find someone like *him* for her to marry.

When the meal finally came to a close Celia was still smiling, chatting easily with Lord Knowlton, and with Lady Helen and her devilishly handsome husband. Servants moved the tables away to make room for dancing as the musicians began tuning their lutes and viols in the gallery above.

"Mistress Sutton, I hope that you will favour me with a pavane," Lord Knowlton said with a bow.

Celia laughed and shook her head. "I fear I have not danced in a very long time. I do not know the latest steps."

And suddenly she recalled exactly when she'd had her last dance—with John Brandon, the night before he'd vanished from her life. It had been a slow Italian passamiento, his hands holding her hard and close as their bodies slid together. He had not smiled as he'd looked down at her in the turns, only stared deeply into her eyes as if to memorise her face. Know her thoughts. She had not yet been betrothed to Sutton then, and had dared to dream the romantic dreams of a young, romantic girl.

She pushed the memory away, buried it deeply with all the others. If only they would cease to work their way free! Cease to make her hope again.

"I do not dance now," she said.

"Then perhaps you will sit with me for a while," Lord Knowlton said. "I find I am loth to lose your company so soon, Mistress Sutton."

Celia made herself smile at him. It felt so unnatural

on her lips, where before it seemed almost easy again. Damn John Brandon anyway. Hadn't he already taken enough? Hadn't she given him enough?

"Only if you will tell me more of those delicious tales you have heard in Edinburgh," she said. "Tell me of the Queen's pet poet over there. They say he is quite in love with her."

As she allowed Lord Knowlton to lead her to one of the benches near the wall she half listened to his voice and tried to summon back the easiness she had felt as they ate together. She nodded and laughed at all the right places, and watched the dancers as they swirled past in the intricate patterns of the dance.

Queen Mary was a graceful dancer, and had an obvious pleasure in the exercise which spread over everyone else. There was much laughter as the men lifted and twirled their partners, skirts flying in a dark, rich pattern. It made Celia wish she could bring herself to dance again. That she could be the girl she had once been, a girl who revelled in music and movement, the feel of a man's arms around her.

One man's arms.

The line of dancers shifted for a moment, and she suddenly saw John standing across the room, as if her memories had summoned him there. For one second it felt as if the years fell away and she saw him for the first time. Her throat tightened, and she felt the pounding of her pulse under the high, tight collar of her gown.

She sat up straighter as his stare focused on her. She couldn't look away, and it seemed that neither could he. His jaw tightened, a muscle flexing in his cheek, and she felt just as she had that very first day. When she'd seen him across a room and something had tightened inside her, pulling her to him. She hadn't been able to explain it then, and she assuredly could not explain it now.

Nor did she want it. She looked away, and when her gaze flickered back to him he was smiling down at a pretty redhead beside him. One of Queen Mary's Marys, who laughed up into his eyes and laid her hand on his arm. He let himself be led away by her, and they vanished into the crowd.

Celia slumped back on her seat, as if the band that held her to John had suddenly been released.

"Are you quite well, Mistress Sutton?" Lord Knowlton asked, his voice concerned. "You look pale."

She shook her head. "I am well, Lord Knowlton. Merely tired, I think. Perhaps I am not entirely recovered from the journey."

"Then let me fetch you some wine."

"Nay, I thank you. I think perhaps I should retire. Queen Mary looks as if she may dance until dawn, and I know I shall fade before then."

Lord Knowlton gently touched her arm. "Shall I escort you?"

His touch made her feel so warm, pleasant—not overwhelmed with desire and need for more. Aye, he would make a fine match for her. If she could summon up more enthusiasm for the notion of marrying again.

"I can find my chamber now, Lord Knowlton," she said. "I would hate for you to miss the dancing. I shall see you tomorrow?"

"Certainly, Mistress Sutton." He kissed her fingertips and let her go with a regretful smile. "Have a good rest."

Celia made her way back through the crowd, which had become noisier and warmer as the night went on. The music was faster, the press of bodies closer. She needed air.

She was almost to the doors when someone caught her hand. She spun around in a sudden panic, ready to slap them with her free hand.

Only to be brought to a skidding halt by John's blue eyes looking straight into hers.

"Going so very soon?" he asked.

Chapter Fourteen

Celia wanted to pull her arm free, turn her back on him and those eyes that saw too much. She wanted to push him away, slap him, force him out of her mind. But she just went very still and gazed back at him. "I am tired. I don't feel like dancing tonight."

"Ah, Celia, but I fear our work is never done. Come, dance with me. There are matters we must discuss."

She glanced over his shoulder, through the doorway to the dancers. The hall seemed even more crowded now, a thick press of people all the way to the far walls. The music was faster, louder.

"I don't remember dancing being a requirement of this task," she said.

"Oh, many things are required of you now, Celia," he answered, with an infuriatingly charming grin. "Come now. One dance. I promise I will not let you fall."

Too late for that, Celia thought wryly as he held out his hand to her. But she was meant to keep a watch over Queen Mary, and that wouldn't be accomplished by running away. Nor could she keep running from John. There was no place far enough away where she could forget him.

She slid her hand into his, and his fingers closed over hers. She felt the heat of his touch, the slight roughness from where he gripped a sword or a jousting lance. His smile widened, and he drew her with him back into the hall.

The last dance had ended, and couples were taking their places for the next as the musicians warmed up for a volta. Queen Mary still led the dance with Lord Darnley, and she seemed not tired at all. A brilliant smile lit her beautiful face, and she clapped her hands together to summon everyone else into the form for the dance.

Celia often forgot how young the Queen actually was: only twenty-two—Celia's own age. A lifetime of being queen had bestowed upon Mary a regal confidence that belied her years, but now, with the pleasure of the dance, she looked young and happy. Whereas Celia felt a hundred years old.

Until John touched her waist and drew her closer to his body. His smile faded as he watched her, his eyes narrowing. His hand tightened, and she felt the press of him through the satin of her bodice, as if he touched her naked skin. His fingers slid around to the small of her back.

Celia licked at her dry lips, and his stare flickered to that small movement. "I haven't danced for a long time," she whispered. "I'm not sure I remember the steps."

"Just follow me and I'll show you the way," he

said. "I'm sure you remember far more than you think you do."

She did. She remembered dancing this same dance with him, laughing merrily as he swung her in the air and drew her close.

The music started, the lively strains washing over her just as they had back then. How she had once loved to dance! How she had revelled in the movement and sound, the energy of the other couples around her. And she had never had another partner like John, never danced with someone else who moved as he did, all lithe, graceful power. They'd danced together then, and did so now, as if their bodies knew each other, moved naturally in perfect unison.

Just the same way their bodies had sex. As if they had always been together, with a warm, delicious intimacy and need. A belonging.

John's hand on her back flexed and he led her into the figures of the dance, smoothly guiding her steps. One, two, sway, turn, leap. She did remember how it went now. She went up on her toes as he spun her under his raised arm, and her feet seemed to tingle with happiness at dancing again.

How many things she had forgotten in life. How many things John was bringing back to her. As she jumped lightly from one foot to the other and turned against him she actually laughed. She lost herself in the moment, the music and movement and his touch, and for a few precious moments it was all she knew. All she wanted.

But all too soon it ended.

She curtsied low as the music spun to a stop, and John bowed. When she looked up he smiled at her.

"You see, Celia," he whispered. "You do still know how to dance."

Only with you, she thought. He was the only one who could ever make her feel like that.

Suddenly his gaze went over her head and sharpened. His hand tightened on hers as he drew her up beside him. Celia glanced back to see Marcus standing in the doorway. Marcus gave a small nod.

"Come with me," John said roughly.

"Where are we going?" she demanded.

"You always ask so many questions," he muttered. "Can you never just trust me?"

Celia feared she was beginning to trust him again too much, and that realisation frightened her to her core. She could not trust John Brandon again, could not open herself to him. The first time had nearly broken her, and her heart had never entirely mended. One blow would surely shatter it beyond redemption.

"Nay," she said. "I cannot."

Still holding onto her hand, he slid a long glance down her body—a look she could swear she felt on her bare skin.

"Are you wearing your dagger?" he asked.

Celia nodded.

"Then if I prove untrustworthy, if I break the trust you give me, pull it out and use it on me," he said. "That should keep me in line."

Celia doubted anything at all could stop him from what he wanted to do. But she followed him out of the crowded hall and into the corridor where Marcus waited. He leaned against the panelled wall, his arms loosely crossed over his chest and a small smile on his face. He looked the image of a lazy, careless courtier, but Celia saw his sharp glance take in her hand in John's.

"News?" John asked.

Marcus shrugged. "Of a sort. Come with me." He led them up a staircase, past couples deep in quiet conversation, and down a narrow corridor to a small closet. The open window let in a cold breeze, flakes of snow, and the only light in the chamber was the silver glow of the moon. It fell on two chairs and an empty fireplace.

"We aren't alone here in Scotland," Marcus said.

"Of course not," John answered. "All of Europe has a stake in Queen Mary's marital plans."

"But I think now one of them may be ready to take action."

Marcus outlined all he had discovered—all the factions aligning against Queen Elizabeth here at Mary's deceptively bright Court. The French Guise family, who didn't want to lose Mary and her royal French connections, the Spanish, who wanted control of Elizabeth's northern neighbour, and Mary herself—so unpredictable.

And the unknown agents who worked for one or all of them.

Celia's head began to ache. She could scarcely fathom what she had found herself embroiled in. And it grew late.

"Let me escort you to your chamber," John said, as if he sensed that she grew weary.

She barely heard Marcus as he made his excuse and left the room, the door sliding shut silently behind him.

Celia felt the light touch of John's hand on her back, just over the lacings of her bodice. She gave him a smile over her shoulder, and prayed she looked far cooler and steadier than she felt. She needed all her wits about her now.

"I do know the way there," she said.

"The hour is very late," he answered. He didn't smile in return, merely watched her, that hand very still on her back.

"I don't think our foes would attack me in the very halls of Queen Mary's palace," Celia said. "I am merely a simple lady-in-waiting, no threat to their plans."

He did smile at that, his mouth flicking up at the corner as that dimple flashed in his cheek. "You were never a simple anything, Celia. But there are drunken men roaming free here, and I don't entirely trust your skill with that dagger."

"Oh, do you not?" Celia whispered. Something about his too-smug tone, the hot touch of his hand on her back, awakened a spirit of mischief in her that had slumbered for too long. She slowly turned, sliding her body against his until she stood pressed to his chest. She slid her palms flat on his abdomen, tracing the hard ridges of his muscles under the brocade doublet. He tensed beneath her touch, and she could see the fire catch in his eyes as he looked down at her.

"Perhaps you would care for a demonstration of

my—skill," she said, and she barely recognised her own voice because it was so low and soft. He made her feel that way, so full of passion and need.

John's arm closed around her back, pulling her up hard against him. "Celia…"

She grasped the slippery, rich fabric of his doublet in her fists and slid it up until she could ease her fingers beneath it and up over his chest. She could feel every hard inch of his body under his thin linen shirt. He felt so strong, so solid under her touch, as if he really could keep her safe. As if she could curl up in his strength and forget the rest of the world for ever.

But who would protect her from him? She had always had more to fear from him than anything else.

And she was so tired of fear. Of always feeling cautious, as if she always walked on a knife's edge of disaster and pain. She drew her hands out from his doublet and flattened them over his heart to push him back against the wall. His other arm came around her waist to trap her to his chest like iron chains. But she wasn't running. Not yet.

She wound her arms around his neck and buried her fingers in the hair that curled over his collar. John drew her up until she was on tiptoe, leaning into him until every inch of their bodies were pressed together.

His erection throbbed against her belly through her skirts, iron-hard. Celia moaned softly and closed her eyes. Her head fell back.

"God's wounds, Celia, but what you do to me," he whispered roughly.

"What *do* I do to you?" she said. Did she drive him

to madness? Drive him out of himself? For that was what he did to her. Had always done to her.

He lowered his head and she felt his lips at her temple, his warm breath stirring her hair, brushing over her skin.

"I don't know if I should kiss you," he muttered, "or tie you to my bed and give you a sound spanking."

Celia gave a startled laugh—and then trembled at the erotic vision his words created in her mind. Herself, bound to John's bed, naked, available to all his desires. She could never trust anyone enough for such games again, never be so helpless, but it was an alluring fantasy.

"I think perhaps we should try both," she said, twisting his hair around her fingers. She gave a sharp tug and pulled his head up. "But I would prefer *you* tied to *my* bed, John Brandon."

"We shall see about that, fairy queen," he growled. Suddenly his mouth slammed down over hers, hard and open, taking what he wanted from her with no quarter given.

Not that Celia wanted to surrender. Not with her own desire rising up within her as if it would obliterate all else. She wanted John, yes, but she didn't want him to obliterate her. To shatter her heart again. She didn't want to be that naive girl any more.

She wanted John as the woman she was now, a woman who knew how cold and desolate the world was and craved the heat of him to drive it all away for a moment. To fall into that warm intimacy that closed around them when they were alone together.

She opened her mouth to his kiss and met the thrust of his tongue with her own, twining with his, tasting him. He tasted like the most wondrous of forbidden nectar, wine and herbs and his own dark essence. She wanted more and more of that.

And he wanted more too. She could feel it in every tense muscle of his body, every hungry thrust of his tongue against hers. She drew harder on his hair as if she could bring him closer, closer, meld him into her. Get drunk on him.

He growled deep in his throat, the primitive, animal sound of it echoing through her body. He pulled her up, up, until he could shove her skirts back and wrap her legs around his waist. Celia braced her arms on his shoulders and tightened her thighs on his hips. Her skirts were tossed up between them, and she felt his penis pressed to her spread pelvis with only the velvet of his breeches between them. She arched into him and he moaned.

Celia laughed, filled with a bright joy that he wanted her, that she could pleasure him. That he was ever so briefly in her power, as he always held her in his. She pressed her legs closer to his hips until he could feel the outline of her dagger, encased in its sheath above her stocking.

"La, John, but I do think you're right," she whispered against his neck. "There *are* men waiting to accost poor ladies-in-waiting in these very corridors. Whatever should I do?"

"Get on your knees and take me into your mouth?" he suggested hopefully.

Celia shook her head and laughed. "Use my dagger on it, mayhap?"

"Witch." He groaned. "You are no fairy queen—'tis obvious now you carry evil magic with you."

Celia pressed her parted lips to his neck, just beneath the hard arch of his jaw. She slid her mouth down the strong, bronzed column, lightly scraping her teeth over the damp skin until she could lick at the pulse pounding at its base. He tasted of salt and wine, of that masculine essence, of John.

She tugged open the jewelled buttons of his doublet and slid the edges apart until she could see a vee of his chest under the loosened shirt lacings. Smooth golden skin overlaid with a rough sprinkling of dark hair.

She nuzzled him there, kissing his skin as she inhaled deeply of his essence. "Then teach me to use it only for good, John."

He groaned, a sound of agonised pleasure deep in his chest, and claimed her mouth again. A hard, desperate kiss, a claiming of lips and tongue that sought to seize something deeper, more profound from her. Celia let her head fall back to her shoulders and surrendered to the emotions that raced through her.

Then she heard a sound, a stumbling footfall outside, a soft laugh that echoed down the corridor. It was quickly silent again, but Celia suddenly knew where they were. What they were doing—what *she* was doing.

She dragged her mouth from John's and sucked in a deep breath of air. She opened her eyes to find him staring down at her, his own eyes dark with desire. She glimpsed a flash of anger deep in their depths.

Anger? She was surely the one who should feel that towards him, this man she should distrust with every fibre of her being and yet who kept drawing her in to him. Closer and closer, until she feared she would fall back into him all over again.

She unwound her legs from his waist and jumped to her feet, so desperate to get away that she stumbled. His hands tightened on her arms, holding her steady.

"Come to my chamber with me now, Celia," he whispered in her ear.

His fingers slid up her arm to her bare shoulder, caressing the skin there until she shivered.

So tempting. She could see how it would be in her mind, the two of them entwined on his bed, skin to skin. But the emotions that went with it were far more frightening.

She shook her head and stumbled back a step from him. His hands fell away from her.

"Not tonight," she said.

"Celia…"

She shook her head again, and spun around to hurry away as fast as her shaking legs could take her. Once she was not with him, once she could take a deep breath that did not smell of him, she'd feel stronger.

He called her a fairy queen, a witch, yet he was the one with a magical spell. He cast it over every woman who came near him, drawing them to him with his smile, his raw aura of power and sensuality. She was no different. Her body knew him, wanted him.

She had to learn to be stronger than her treacherous body. Her heart.

Celia turned onto the narrow corridor that led to her small chamber. It was dark, the only light one torch that glowed in its sconce at the far end. A cold draught raced along the stone floors and she hurried her steps. She wanted to be safely in her chamber, alone.

A soft sound brought her to a halt. She stood poised on tiptoe, every sense alert. She had dismissed John and Marcus's warnings about enemies, since she was too insignificant in this game of queens to be in any danger, but she suddenly felt on edge. This was a strange night, and Holyrood was a strange place. Surely anything could happen.

She grasped her skirts in one hand, ready to draw them up and pull out her dagger. Carefully, she backed towards the wall and glanced around her, holding her breath.

She let out a sigh when she saw the source of that sound. Marcus and Allison stood entwined in the embrasure of a doorway, kissing. Her hands were pushing his doublet off his shoulders as his delved into her bodice. Their bright hair, golden and red, gleamed in the torchlight.

Celia bit her lip to keep from laughing. Perhaps there had been a potion in the wine tonight—one that turned anyone who drank of it lustful.

Marcus reached behind Allison to open the door, and they fell together into the chamber. Celia was alone again. And she wasted no time in finding her own room and locking the door behind her. She had had enough of the enchantments of the night.

Chapter Fifteen

Celia half-listened to Mary Fleming, one of Queen Mary's Marys, as she sang a French ballad and softly played the lute. She was accompanied by giggles and whispered conversations, the rustle of silken skirts and the brush of needle and thread against cloth. It was such a feminine scene: Queen Mary's ladies all gathered around her in her chamber during a long, cold afternoon. A scene fragrant with French perfumes and powders, the rose oil in the burners set in the corners, the sweetness from platters of honey cakes.

But Celia's thoughts lingered far away, on a very masculine object. What did he do today? Was he angry she had left him so dissatisfied last night? She hadn't been able to read the swirl of emotions in his eyes.

She stabbed her needle hard into the cloth she held. She did not care what he did, what he thought. Not now, in the harsh light of day.

She really did not. She did *not*. Only she knew she did—far too much.

"Ouch!" She gasped as her needle caught the tip of her finger. As she raised it to her lips to soothe the sting she saw Lady Allison watching her. Allison gave her a little smile and looked back to her own work.

Celia saw that she had sewn the edges of the sleeve she worked on together and would now have to unpick them. She glanced over at Queen Mary, who sat by the window with her embroidery frame, her little dogs gathered around her footstool. Unlike Celia, the Queen obviously enjoyed her needlework and was very skilled at it. She moved the gold thread slowly in and out, humming along with the song, a smile playing over her lips.

Celia had been surprised to receive a summons from the Queen that morning to join her ladies in the Queen's apartments. She had been sure it would take longer to work her way into Mary's company, her trust. But the Scottish Queen seemed to have none of Queen Elizabeth's caution. She was all open, friendly smiles, greeting Celia as she arrived, asking her questions about England and her English cousin, making sure she met all the ladies.

But there had as yet been no talk at all about Mary's marital intentions.

Celia lowered the mangled sleeve to her lap and examined the chamber around her. It was not the grand, opulent space she would have expected, this chamber high up in one of the towers. It was reached only by a narrow spiral staircase, and had a low ceiling of compartmented panels, covered with the entwined initials of Mary's parents, King James and Marie of Guise. Despite the large windows, looking out on the nearby abbey, and the large fireplace filled with bright flames, the room felt small and dark.

Celia glanced through one open doorway to the outer chamber, where the Queen's guards waited, and then through another, half-closed door into a tiny, octagonal supper room. Behind her was the Queen's bed, a massive, carved edifice hung with red curtains. It all felt very intimate and small.

Surely not what Mary had been used to in France.

"They say the Queen's chief adviser Lord Maitland is in love with her," Allison suddenly whispered to Celia.

Celia glanced up, startled. "In love with the Queen? That's not surprising—every man seems to be."

Allison laughed. "Mayhap not *every* man. But Maitland is also in love with Mary Fleming, despite the fact that he is at least twenty years older than her. They say the Queen is planning a lavish wedding for them."

"Is she?" Celia murmured.

"Don't you remember, Mistress Sutton? The Queen's Marys vowed never to wed until *she* did. If one of them is soon to marry…"

Celia looked sharply to the Queen, who was laughing at her dogs' gambols. "Who?"

"Who do you think?" Allison whispered with a giggle.

Suddenly Mary clapped her hands, drawing everyone's attention to her. "It is such a dull, grey day," she said merrily, in her musical French accent. "I think we need to liven things up a bit."

Mary Fleming clapped her hands in answer. "Your Grace! Do you mean…?"

"I do," the Queen said happily. "It has been much too long, *n'est-ce pas?*"

All the Queen's French ladies laughed. Celia watched them uncertainly.

"Mistress Sutton, Lady Allison—perhaps you would join us?" Queen Mary called. "I'm sure you would enjoy it very much."

Celia could not help but wonder how she found herself in such predicaments when she tried to live so cautiously.

On the other hand, perhaps she had had enough of caution. Sometimes freedom was so much more enjoyable. She had never felt quite like this before.

Celia caught a glimpse of herself reflected in an icy puddle on the street as she followed Queen Mary and a few of her ladies through the shadowy lanes. She hardly recognised herself. She wore a pair of velvet breeches and tall boots, with a man's velvet and wool doublet and a short cloak, all in green embroidered with gold. Her hair was pinned up tightly and covered with a plumed cap she had tugged low on her brow. With her slender figure she could pass for a young man, if no one looked too closely.

She looked like her brother, as she remembered him when he was alive. Slim and dark-haired.

But she did not want to think of her brother and what had happened to him in the end, of his stupidity. Not today, when she actually felt the hum of excitement in her blood, the warmth of dangerous life. The only other time she had felt that of late had been in bed with John.

Or in the corridor, with her legs around his waist…

She pushed away the heated memory of the night before, losing herself in John's kiss, and hurried after the Queen. Queen Mary was also dressed in men's clothes, rich crimson and black, and with her tall figure she was far more convincing as a male than Celia. She held the arm of Mary Fleming, who wore her own gown and cloak, and the two of them laughed together as if they were in a conspiracy.

And so they were. So they all were now.

Celia glanced at Lady Helen McKerrigan, who walked beside her. Helen also wore men's garments, but she moved in them more easily than Celia. She looked as if she had done this before. With the Queen— or perhaps as a game with her handsome, broodingly dark husband?

Celia wondered what John would think of her in these clothes. Would his eyes darken, as they always did when he was aroused? Would he reach for her, his hard fingers sliding into her breeches, his blue eyes burning with emotion…

Stop it! she told herself sternly. She needed to cease this at once. Such thoughts were too dangerous.

"Does Queen Mary do this often?" she whispered to Helen.

Helen smiled. "Not as often as she would like, I think. But sometimes, when life at Holyrood becomes too serious for her. It's never easy living between her Scots courtiers and her French friends."

Celia nodded. She had certainly seen the great tension between the two factions, the way Queen Mary trod carefully between the two. "And no one recognises her?"

Helen laughed. "No one says anything to her, at least. She wanders where she will on these days. I think she hopes to hear unguarded gossip in the streets and taverns."

"And does she hear such things?"

A clutch of Puritan clergymen in their stark black garments appeared on the front steps of a chapel as Queen Mary passed by, laughing merrily. Their grey faces were pinched with disapproval, and one made a gesture after her.

"Sometimes she hears more than she would care to," Helen murmured. "The Queen was gone from Scotland for a very long time. Some don't care for a French Catholic monarch."

They hurried after Mary as she turned down a narrow lane. The cobbles were cracked and broken under their feet, the humid smell of rotting food and human waste sharper. Celia pulled out a scented handkerchief and walked faster.

"But we should speak of more pleasant matters!" Helen said, taking Celia's arm as they walked. "What is happening with you and that handsome Sir John?"

Celia gave her a startled glance, suddenly filled with uncertainty. Was it all so obvious that now she was an object of gossip? "What do you mean?"

Helen laughed. "I have seen how he looks at you. It's quite delicious. How could any woman resist?"

"Aren't you married, Lady Helen?" Celia said, remembering Helen's handsome husband and the way he always watched his wife with such love in his eyes.

Helen just laughed louder, drawing glances from passers-by. "Very much so, and my husband keeps me very happy indeed. But I can still look, can I not? And I fear I am a terrible romantic. My husband teases me about it. He says I want life to be like a troubadour's ballad."

"Sometimes life is far too much like a ballad," Celia murmured, remembering the feelings that swept over her whenever she was near John.

"Is it?"

"I prefer matters to be more peaceful."

"But that is so dull!" Helen protested. "Who wants peace when a man like Sir John looks at you as if he wants to eat you up right then and there?"

Celia laughed. "Does he?" She had to admit the thought of John looking at her like that, of being devoured by him, was not entirely unpleasant.

"Yes. Right then and there." Helen's hand tightened on Celia's arm and she drew her closer. "Such intensity from a man can be frightening, I know. I tried to run from my husband at first as well. But surely not to give in to those feelings, not to live fully, is worse?"

Celia shook her head. "You don't understand. I gave in once. It did not end well."

Helen gave her a long, searching look. "And ending can change. It did for me and my James."

"It cannot for me," Celia said firmly. But her emotions were far more confused.

Helen looked as if she wanted to say more, but Queen

Mary suddenly veered off through an open doorway and they had to follow. There was no time for more conversation.

Helen's words lingered with Celia. Better to give in to feelings, to live fully. Once Celia would have completely agreed with her—until her feelings had crushed her. Now...

Now she didn't know how she felt. Not really. She wanted John, but did she dare to trust him? Trust the way he was making her feel again?

Queen Mary had led them into a tavern, a cheap, dark place with scarred tables and a sticky, warped wooden floor. A fire smoked in the grate, and the smell of ale and stewed onions was thick in the air. It was crowded even at that hour, with a rough group who seemed deep in their cups. Any talk here was low-pitched, and stares followed them as they passed.

Celia rested her gloved hand on the hilt of the short sword at her waist, ready to draw it at the slightest hint of trouble.

Mary seemed to notice nothing. She strode confidently through the room to an empty table in the corner. She waved them all to sit down around her and called for ale as she drew Celia to the chair right next to hers.

"My dear Madame Sutton," Mary whispered, in that confiding voice that drew so many people to her. "You must tell me more about Lord Darnley."

Celia looked at the Queen in shock. "I—me, Your Grace? I have never spoken to him."

Mary smiled. "But you live at my cousin's Court.

And you were on this long journey here, yes? I know you watch people, see things."

Celia took a quick gulp of her ale. She hardly knew what to say. She could scarcely tell this queen, this woman with her wide, glowing amber eyes, the truth. Not until she was sure of what Queen Elizabeth would want.

"They say he is exceedingly handsome, Your Grace," she said carefully.

Mary laughed—a silvery sound that made everyone around them laugh too. "I do see that, Madame Sutton! Very well. But what of his affections? Are they engaged?"

Celia was saved by a burst of song, too loud to talk over, and Mary turned to clap along to the tune. Celia looked away as well, but she knew it was only a short reprieve. Mary would ask her again, and she would have to know what to say.

Suddenly a hidden door opened across the room and shadowy figures appeared there. Still laughing at the bawdy song, Celia turned to study the newcomers over the edge of her tankard.

She froze before she could take a sip. *John* was standing there, staring right back at her with those blazing blue eyes. She carefully lowered the ale back to the table before she could spill any.

Marcus appeared at John's shoulder as several men she did not recognise slipped past and out of the tavern. John spoke quietly to Marcus, his gaze never leaving her. She found she was caught by that stare and couldn't turn away.

What was he doing here? A meeting at such a tavern surely seemed to bode ill. Was he in some conspiracy she knew nothing about? She had had quite enough of conspiracies of late.

He came towards her slowly, deliberately, dodging around the crowded tables. He still watched her, his eyes narrowed.

"Sir John! Lord Marcus!" Queen Mary cried brightly. "Come and join us. We were just teaching our English friends some Parisian songs."

"Such a surprise to see you all here," Marcus said, as smoothly as if finding a queen dressed like a man in a rough tavern happened all the time. "And a charming surprise at that. You've brightened a very dull day."

"You look as if your days are never dull, Lord Marcus," Mary Fleming teased. "Do you know any good songs?"

"I just might know one or two," he said, sliding onto the seat by Mary Fleming and wrapping his arm around her shoulders. "None as fine as yours, though."

John took the chair next to Celia when Lady Helen obligingly slid down. Celia watched him warily as he removed the tankard from her suddenly cold fingers and raised it to his mouth. With a flick of his wrist he turned it and drank from the spot where her lips had been. The smooth muscles of his neck above the open collar of his doublet shifted as he swallowed, and Celia had to look away.

"Do *you* know any French songs from your time in Paris?" she said.

"None I would teach to you."

"Oh? Why is that? Because I have such a wretched voice?"

"Because they are all naughty, Celia, and I don't think I could take hearing you say those words with your pretty mouth," he said roughly, and drank deeply again. "You have me too lustful as it is."

Celia was surprised he would admit it. *She* would never give *him* that power, even though she seemed to burst into desire every time they touched. She caught a glimpse of Lady Helen from the corner of her eye, and Helen grinned at her.

Celia almost laughed aloud. Maybe it was the clothes she wore, the ale she was drinking, but she felt a sudden surge of some strange power wash through her. She did not feel quite like herself.

She reached for the ale and took a long gulp. "Words like swive? Or tup? Or maybe…" She whispered a word in his ear she had never said aloud.

John growled low in his throat. "Celia…"

She put down the tankard and slowly eased her hand down below the concealment of the table. She felt his thigh beneath her fingertips, his lean muscles bunching and shifting under her teasing touch. She trailed her fingers up slowly, slowly, the wool of his breeches a soft friction on her skin.

Just as she brushed his codpiece he seized her wrist and held her away. But he didn't put her hand back on the table, merely held it there, a mere inch from his manhood. She could feel its hardness, his desire, could see that need in his eyes.

"What game do you play, Celia?" he demanded, his voice low.

"The Queen commanded me to accompany her today," Celia said, flexing her fingers. "I could hardly refuse."

"I don't mean appearing here in these clothes," he answered. His bright blue stare swept over her slowly, taking in every inch of her body in the form-fitting clothes until it felt as if he caressed her. "Though you do look tempting. I want to—"

"Sir John!" Queen Mary suddenly called. "Lord Marcus tells us you do know some songs. Teach us one now."

John gave Celia one more long look—a hard glance that promised their conversation was not nearly over. Then he turned to smile at Mary, pressing his body against Celia's shoulder.

"Of course," he said. "Your wish is my command. What is your pleasure tonight? A comic song? One of adventure? Or one of romance?"

Mary sighed. "Oh, romance! I do love a love song the very best. What is life without love?"

Chapter Sixteen

John followed Celia closely as they made their way back through the streets of Edinburgh to the palace. Night was gathering around them now, shadows seeping down over the steep roofs and flowing over the wet cobblestones. Queen Mary was laughing with her friends, all of them a bit unsteady on their feet after an afternoon of tavern ale and bawdy songs.

Celia and John brought up the end of the group, and she was quiet, thoughtful, as if she wasn't really there in the winter streets. She so often seemed somewhere else, somewhere deep in her own mind, her own sadness, where he couldn't reach her. Couldn't know her, possess her. Not as he feared he wanted to. He wanted so many things from Celia, wanted to give her so much.

He wrapped his fist over the hilt of his sword to keep from caressing her firm, high backside so enticingly outlined in those breeches. He became aroused just watching her, smelling her perfume. He always wanted her. Sex had always been so easy for them—

explosive, undeniable. But the sex had also led to so much more, to tenderness and need.

It had been everything else that drove them apart.

Celia glanced over her shoulder at him, and her eyes widened when she saw the desire that must be blazing in his eyes. A slow pink blush spread across her cheeks, making him want her even more. He wanted to seize her around the waist, push her up against the wall and feel her legs wrap around him, her mouth open under his...

A smile quirked her lips and she reached back to secretly brush her hand over his clenched fist. It was a soft, fleeting touch, a secret smile, and it made something clench deep in his chest. Something warm and tender that he remembered so well with her, only felt with her.

A burst of laughter from up ahead drew her attention away, and she turned from him. Without those cool grey eyes searching his face that tight feeling eased and he sucked in a deep breath. But he stayed close to her as she hurried to catch up to the others.

"Ah, but Sir John must remember the Elysee gardens, since he was so lately in Paris!" Queen Mary cried. "Where are you, Sir John? Come and talk with us!"

"I am here, Your Grace," he answered.

"You must tell them how lovely the gardens are. I want to recreate their pathways and groves here at Holyrood, to remind me of Paris," the Queen said. "If only I could see it again—"

Suddenly the night was shattered by a deafening blast. Up ahead the dark sky lit up red and orange, with flames that shot high above the rooftops. Screams and cries broke out. John barely glimpsed Marcus shoving Queen Mary to the wall before he himself grabbed Celia up in his arms and arched his body over hers to protect her from the sparks that showered down.

She trembled in his arms, her hands curling hard into his doublet as she clung to him. "What is it?" she gasped.

"I don't know," he said, feeling only the primitive drive to protect her, keep her safe. "We need to get to the palace. Now."

Holding her under his arm, he ran behind the others until they burst out of the maze of streets and found the gates of Holyrood. The Queen's guards were already gathered there, halberds at the ready. There was barely a glimpse of a building ablaze somewhere in the city below.

The Queen, looking pale and startled but composed, was borne into the palace.

John tried to set Celia on her feet, to steady her, but she still held onto him.

"What was that?" she whispered. "It all happened so very fast…"

"Shh, you're safe now," he answered. He kissed her hair, her cheek, felt the warmth of her under his lips, the precious life of her—life that was very fragile. He held her now, kept her safe with him. But for how much longer?

"I do not feel safe," she said, her voice unsteady, breathless. "I never feel safe. Not since—since…"

Since her brother's death. The death John had helped hasten. He held her even closer.

"John," he heard Marcus say softly. John looked over Celia's head to see his friend's grim face, his gesture towards the doors.

"Celia, I must go now—find out what has happened," John whispered in her ear. "Go and see to the Queen. I will find you later."

He kissed her once more and gently set her away from him. She nodded. Her face was white and strained, her eyes bright, but she did not cry. He had never seen her cry.

She hurried to the stairs, and John watched her go until she was out of his sight and gone from him.

Chapter Seventeen

Celia slowly paced to the end of her small bedchamber and back again, one deliberate step after another. It was very late, and the whole palace seemed silent and still even after the clamor of the afternoon. The Queen had insisted on dancing again, pretending nothing had happened, but now even she had retired.

Celia knew she should go to bed as well. There was to be a hunt in the morning and they would ride out early. But she knew that even if she lay on the bed, crawled beneath the inviting blankets and closed her eyes, she would not sleep.

John had not been at supper, had not appeared for the dancing. She hadn't seen him since he'd left her by the doors.

She closed her eyes and drew her fur-trimmed robe closer around her as she tried to force away the worry and uncertainty. She could still feel the way his arms had closed around her as the sky exploded, the way he'd shielded her with his body and she'd felt his heart thunder in his chest. The way she trusted him to keep her safe.

Trusted him.

But who would keep *him* safe now, wherever he had gone? Would he vanish from her again? Would she be left to mend her heart all over again? Because she feared her feelings now were stronger than they ever had been before.

Celia shuddered and clutched tighter to the folds of her robe. She wanted to run away from him, as far and as fast as she could. Yet even stronger was the urge to run *to* him, to touch him again and know he was there, alive and real and hers.

Only he was not hers. He never had been.

A quiet knock suddenly sounded at her door, and Celia gasped at the sound. She whirled around, reaching for her dagger where it lay on the table. The noise breaking the heavy silence had pulled her senses taut.

"Wh-what is it?" she called.

"'Tis me, Celia. For pity's sake let me in."

Her fingers convulsed on the dagger's cold hilt. *John.* It was John, here, right when her longing for him was too great. She wanted to send him away; she wanted to throw open the door and catch him in her arms.

She carefully set the dagger back down and took a deep breath before she crossed the floor to unbolt the door.

He stood there in his shirtsleeves, his arms braced on the door frame. He smelled faintly of smoke, and she glimpsed a dark smudge on his bristled cheek. His eyes were hooded, veiled as he stared down at her.

"What has happened?" Celia whispered.

In answer, he closed his arms hard around her and lifted her into the room. He kicked the door closed behind him, and her single candle flickered and went out, enclosing them in darkness.

"John…" she said, but her words died in her throat as his mouth came down over hers. His tongue pressed roughly past her lips, hungry, desperate.

Celia felt an answering need swell inside her, driving out everything else but him. But the thought that she could have lost him for ever drove her on. She felt his hands hungrily push her robe back from her shoulders and onto the floor, felt his fingers tear at the lacings of her chemise and strip the last thin layer of cloth from her body, leaving her naked. She didn't care, didn't want to shield herself from him. She only wanted his touch on her, everywhere.

One of his hands drove into her hair, angling her head for his kiss, while the other swept in a hard caress down her back to the curve of her backside. His fingers dug into the soft skin as he dragged her closer to his body.

She went up on her toes and wound her arms around his neck, cradling his head as she opened her mouth wider to his tongue. He groaned against her, and she felt his erection grow even harder against her bare stomach through his breeches. She arched into it.

John's hand slid to her thigh and lifted her up higher, until her legs wrapped around his hips. She held close, lost in a sizzling haze of sensation, of his touch, his kiss, his body wrapped around hers.

His hand tightened on her leg, and one of his long fingers touched her between her legs, pressing into her damp folds. She cried out at the bolt of pleasure and her head tilted back.

He used his hand in her hair to draw her back even further, leaving her neck vulnerable to his seeking mouth. It slid, open and wet, down her throat until he closed his teeth hard on the soft curve just above her shoulder.

"John!" she cried.

"Do you want me, Celia?" he whispered against her skin.

The tip of his tongue licked at the sting of his bite and a tremble swept through her with the longing.

"Tell me you want me as much as I want you."

Want him? Whatever she was feeling now, whatever was making her damaged heart crack wide open, it went far beyond mere want. It went into sheer need, tenderness she could not fathom.

"I do want you," she said. His mouth slid lower and closed over her aching nipple, sucking it deep. "God's blood, but I want you!"

He backed her up until he could lie her on the bed, amid the soft velvet blankets. As he stepped back her legs slid from his hips, and she almost cried out at the chill of loss. But he merely stripped away his own clothes, ripping them off and tossing them away before catching her up in his arms again.

Their mouths clashed in a heated kiss, and the very air around her seemed to turn warm and heavy, as before a storm. That storm raged inside her, violent and powerful as everything she had locked away and suppressed for three long years broke free and threatened to drown her. She held onto John and let herself go under, let herself feel again at long last.

He pulled his mouth from hers, making her moan with the loss, but he did not leave her. His hands held onto her hips, so tight she felt almost bruised, yet she didn't care. She needed that hardness, that edge of pain and passion that told her he was with her, they were alive together. And soon he would be inside her, making him hers even if only for the night.

They knelt facing each other in the middle of the bed. He let go of her for an instant to untie the bed curtains, enclosing them in their own tiny world with red velvet, shutting away everything but the two of them. Then he reached for her again and slid her close to his naked chest.

Celia laid her palms over the curve of his shoulders. "So beautiful," she whispered. That smooth, damp skin over his lean muscles, so perfect but for a white scar arcing over his ribs, a crescent on his hip. She let her hands slide slowly, slowly down his chest, feeling every inch of him, every taut shift and ripple of his skin. He held her lightly by her hips, letting her explore him.

The light whorls of hair sprinkled across his chest tickled her skin and made her smile. The smile faded as her fingertips slid over the flat discs of his nipples. Her nail scraped over one and it went taut as he groaned. His head fell back, his eyes closed, and she felt his penis jerk where it was pressed to her abdomen.

She lowered her head and took that pebbled nipple

into her mouth, sucking, biting as he held onto her. She could feel the heavy beat of his heart on her lips, the ragged rhythm of his breath. His hands convulsed on her hips. She let her fingers trace down his chest lower, lower, over his ridged stomach to the arrow of hair from his navel to his manhood, the hard line of his hips.

Her open mouth followed the path of her touch, licking, caressing, tasting him. As she bit at the arc of his hip she let her hand flutter over his penis. It was hot satin stretched taut over rigid steel, the veins etched on it pulsating with his need. His need for *her*, for what she was doing to him now, and that realisation flooded her with a powerful pleasure.

She pressed her lips to his taut stomach as she ran her hand down the length of him and up again to its base. She caressed that spot just behind that she knew he liked.

"Celia!" he shouted. He drove his hand into her hair again and pressed her against him.

She smiled and trailed her mouth lower, until she could slip the tip of him between her lips. He tasted sweet and musky, his skin burning as she slowly took him deeper. When her husband had made her do this it had made her feel so ashamed, ill. But now, with John, with her own choice, it made her feel so very different. So in control. She could give *him* pleasure in return for what he gave her, and it felt glorious.

"Celia," he said, his voice no more than a rough growl. His hand slid through her hair and she ran her tongue over him. His hips twitched but he didn't push himself deeper.

She slid her hands around to his tight buttocks and held him to her as she caressed that warm skin, the curve at the small of his back. His hips thrust against her.

Suddenly he caught her shoulders and pushed her back from him. Celia tilted her head to look up at him, and in the red shadows of their bed his face looked harsh, carved into hard lines with lustful need.

"I can't bear it any more, Celia," he said, and pulled her up to kiss her. There was no seductive art to his kiss now, only hunger and a raw lust that called out to her own desire.

She wrapped her arms around him as they fell back onto the bed. John rolled her beneath him, his hips between her spread thighs as he kissed her jaw, the soft, vulnerable spot beneath her ear. He bit down on the curve of her neck, and she cried out as she arched against him. The pain and pleasure sparkled through her.

He trailed his open-mouthed kiss lower, tasting her with his tongue until he captured her aching nipple between his lips and suckled her, rolling her between his teeth.

"John, John," she cried. She cradled his head in her hands, holding him against her. Her whole body felt so *alive*, burning with need for him and what he was doing to her. What only he could do to her.

His hand drove between her thighs and traced her wet seam before he dipped one finger inside her, pressing deep. His palm rotated over that tiny spot of pure sensation, moving over her as he slid in another finger.

He plunged deeper, harder, just the way she needed right now.

He always seemed to know just what she needed, what she wanted, as if he could see into her very heart.

She shook away that disturbing thought, that knowledge that he could know her as no one else ever could, and just let herself feel. Let herself be with him.

But he seemed to sense that instant of disquiet. His hand slid away from her and he held onto her waist as he rolled beneath her and held her on top of him, strong and steady.

He turned her away from him, astride his hips, and traced his touch down the length of her back over her buttocks.

"Ride me, Celia," he commanded.

She laughed at the heady rush of his words and rested her hands behind her on his thighs as she raised herself up and slowly lowered onto his erect penis, one inch at a time. She let him slide deeper, deeper, until he was fully inside her, joined to her. She closed her eyes and let her head drop back as she revelled in the sensation of being filled by him. Part of him.

He wound the ends of her hair around his wrist and thrust his hips up beneath her.

She let her need take her over and moved on top of him faster, harder, until they were moving as one. She felt that hot pressure build from where he touched her, slid against her. It expanded inside her, up and up, until it exploded.

She cried out her pleasure, her back arching like a taut bowstring over his body.

"Celia!" he shouted, and she felt him go still and rigid beneath her, felt the heat of his release inside of her.

The energy drained slowly out of her, leaving her weak and shivering. She collapsed beside him to the bed and listened to the harsh, unsteady rhythm of his breath.

He reached for her and drew her to his side as he covered them both with the bedclothes. In the darkness behind the curtains she knew only the soft touch of his hand in her hair, the sound of his body shifting on the pillows. Her own thoughts were a confused jumble in her tired mind.

She rolled onto her side and let him cradle her against him as she closed her eyes. She needed to rest—just for a moment…

Celia slowly swam up from beneath her hazy dreams, becoming aware of the world around her again. She fought against waking up as her dream had been a sweet one of lying in a warm summer meadow as John kissed her. The sun had streamed down over her in the vision, hot and golden, melting away the long winter, and she had been laughing with John, happy in his arms, lazy and content.

Now she could feel the cold again, the draughts of the old castle pressing against the bed curtains. She blinked her eyes open to find herself lying on her side, surrounded by darkness, the blankets drawn up over her breasts.

And John's mouth on her bare shoulder.

His arm was heavy over her waist, drawing her back

against him. His lips were lazy, slowly exploring her skin, but the sensation that kiss evoked in her was not contentment.

He awoke a restlessness in her, a need that she could feel in the sudden dampness between her legs. He had brought her such pleasure in the night, moments when all thoughts and worries flew away and she could be free. Now sanity was trying to return, to remind her of who they were and all that had happened, but his kiss drove them away again.

"You're awake, Celia," he murmured. "I can feel it." He swept her hair over her shoulder and pressed his mouth to the vulnerable nape of her neck.

She slid herself closer to him and felt the unmistakable proof of his desire, hard against her backside. "So are you."

John laughed roughly. "I have been for some time. But I wanted to hold you in my arms while you slept."

"Why?" she asked, a ridiculous hope blooming deep in her heart.

"Because there are no daggers or sharp words while you dream. You were actually smiling. What did you see there?"

"A world with no snow," she answered.

"And no games of queens and thrones?"

"That would be too much to ask for." Celia laid her hand on the arm over her waist and slowly trailed her fingertips over his warm skin. She felt the soft brush of his hair, the strength of his muscles. She remembered how he had snatched her up in his arms and held her safe amidst the explosion. How she had felt safe with him even in the midst of chaos.

"Did you and Marcus discover what happened today?" she asked.

For an instant he grew tense against her, before drawing her closer and relaxing again. "It was nothing. Merely a young hothead of a Puritan, a disciple of Queen Mary's great enemy Knox. He thought an abandoned building at the edge of the city was being readied to be made into a Catholic chapel so he set it afire. Unfortunately barrels of whisky were stored there for a tavern down the street and the place exploded."

"Was it really going to be a chapel?"

"Certainly not. The only Catholic chapel left in Scotland, aside from secret ones, is the Queen's own, here at Holyrood. She has declared that Protestantism will remain the faith of Scotland even as she follows her own faith privately."

"Was the man captured?"

"Aye. But there are plenty to take his place."

Celia trailed her fingers along his arm again, thinking of all the trouble, all the evil that lurked in the world. The grave danger of coming into the orbit of princes. Her poor brother had learned that lesson all too well, and here she was in Scotland, surrounded by things she only half understood.

"And will the Queen marry soon?" she asked.

"Almost certainly. She is not the sort of woman who can be long without a man."

"Darnley?"

"Aye."

"But why?" Celia asked. "He is the veriest knave. And she is a queen."

"A queen with few options. There are few eligible princes of her rank in Europe, and her pride won't let her wed a subject."

"Queen Elizabeth has offered Leicester."

John laughed. "Mary is a woman of pride—a great deal of it. She won't take her cousin's man."

"So that leaves Darnley." Celia had never thought she could pity a queen—not in her own impoverished, homeless state. And yet she found she did. She pitied Mary and Elizabeth both, trapped by their lives. They would never know a feeling like she had with John, and even when she knew she should not feel that way she could not let it go.

"Mary does not see Darnley as we do," John said.

"Does she not?"

"Nay." He wound a long strand of her hair around his wrist, running it between his fingers. "I have learned a great deal about people in my life, Celia. How to read them, how to guess what they will do next."

"About women?" She knew he could read women all too easily, their secret needs and desires.

He gave a humourless laugh. "Aye, about women. Though some are harder to understand than others." His arm tightened around her. "Some I can't fathom at all."

"And Queen Mary?"

"Even though she grew up at the French Court, a viper pit if there ever was one, she is terrible at prevarication. She wears her heart on her sleeve, her emotions at the surface. She is very impulsive. And she is lonely. She has been a widow for a long time."

"And Darnley is handsome," Celia said. But she knew too well what happened when a woman looked beyond a handsome face.

"He is, and charming when he wants to be. And, as Mary's cousin, he is nearly as close to the English throne as she is. It is all she can see now. The surface." He released her hair and smoothed it over her shoulder. "But after she weds him she will soon come to regret it. He will not be a strong consort for her."

Aye, Celia no longer envied queens at all. And she was suddenly weary of them and their labyrinthine doings. She only wanted John right now, and the way he made her feel. She rolled over to face John and sat up on the bed, letting the blanket fall to her waist.

"What about me, John?" she said. "What can you read about me?"

He reached out to wrap his fingers over the curve of her hip and drew her closer to him. "You, Celia—you drive me mad," he muttered. He pressed his open mouth to her belly, just below her navel. "I want to know you, to see you, but you keep slipping away from me."

Celia wove her fingers through his tousled hair and held him against her. Her head fell back and she closed her eyes as she let the pleasure of his kiss wash over her. Perhaps she did understand something of what drove Queen Mary onward to disaster—she missed *this*, this sensual haze created only by a lover's caress. The heat of a kiss, another person nearby in the darkness. A man and a woman and the mystery of what happened between them.

His fingers tightened on her buttocks and he drew her closer to his mouth. He dipped the tip of his tongue into her navel and traced it lower over her abdomen in a hot, sinuous pattern. It was a slow, careful touch, as if he branded her skin with his tongue and marked her for ever.

Behind her closed eyes she felt him slide lower on the bed, until his mouth was over her womanhood. He laid her down flat on the pillows and parted her legs. He blew a soft breath over her and she gasped at the ripple of sensation. She ached for more, but he merely touched his mouth lightly to her damp opening.

"John…" she whispered brokenly.

Then his tongue slid over her, licked her slowly up and down before he plunged into her. He tasted her deeply. His fingertips caressed that tiny spot just above and pleasure overwhelmed her. She arched up into his mouth, holding onto his hair as he kissed her *there*, deeper and deeper.

He took her leg and draped it over his shoulder, so he could slide even deeper between her legs. Somehow it felt even more intimate than when they coupled, as if he could see into her soul, become part of her. And she did not even care. She wanted him there, in every part of her. Needed him there.

He pinched lightly at that spot and speared his tongue into her hard, making her cry out as a climax built in her core. It broke over her, and John groaned against her, making the feeling even more intense.

As she floated back to earth he kissed her once more, softly, and rose up on his knees between her legs. She saw him smile in the shadows, saw him raise his fingers to his mouth as he tasted her again on his skin.

Lust and emotion spasmed deep inside her all over again.

"So sweet," he said, and leaned down to bury his face in the side of her neck, in the tangle of hair that fell over her shoulder. He just held her there, inhaled the scent of her hair as if he would draw her into him.

Celia felt a terrible longing envelop her, and she wrapped her arms around his back. His skin was damp, sleek, and he shifted under her touch.

"Celia, Celia," he whispered into her hair.

Just her name, over and over.

It made her want to weep. Never to let him go.

He sat up and drew her with him until she straddled his lap, her legs spread over him. She felt his erect manhood slide against her, and wanted him all over again. She raised herself up on her knees and reached down to guide him into place, so she could slowly lower herself onto him.

He groaned and thrust his hips up until he was fully inside her, their hips pressed together, her legs wrapped tight around his waist. She let her head fall forward onto his shoulder, and it felt as if they were one being.

He drew back and thrust up again, a long, slow slide. She could feel every inch of him move against her, inside her. She rose up as he drew back, and then down, finding their rhythm together again. Even their breath, their heartbeats, matched.

He growled, and his hands closed tightly on her waist as they moved faster, rougher. He thrust up into her hard, his hips grinding against hers, circling.

"John," she gasped. Her nails dug into his shoulders as she matched him thrust for thrust. Her breasts slid over his chest, their legs tangled together, and she couldn't breathe, couldn't think, could only move. Could only slide her body over his as he thrust against that one pleasurable spot over and over.

"John!" she cried as she flew apart all over again.

He threw his head back, the veins in his neck taut, his eyes closed as he pushed into her one more time. "Celia," he moaned.

Her name had never sounded quite like that before.

They sank down to the bed, arms and legs still entwined. John drew her down on top of him, her body stretched out over his as her head rested on his shoulder. His hand moved slowly through her hair, a gentle caress over and over, soothing her pounding heart.

She couldn't say anything. She had no words any longer. She could only hold onto him as she spiraled ever downward.

Chapter Eighteen

Celia had to hold her hand over her mouth to keep from laughing as she trailed behind the others from the church after the lengthy—and loud—service. Darnley felt he had to attend John Knox's Protestant services to establish his religious allegiances in Scotland, and Celia and the others went to keep an eye on him. She wished she could have stayed at Holyrood, or was back at Whitehall with Elizabeth's clergymen's short, simple sermons. Knox had railed against the "horrors" of female rule until Celia had feared she would collapse in giggles. Poor Queen Mary—she would surely soon wish she had stayed in France.

She was so deep in her own thoughts she didn't realise anyone had moved to walk beside her until she felt a gentle touch on her arm. She looked up, startled, to see Lord Knowlton smiling at her.

"It makes one miss Queen Elizabeth's less devout clergymen, does it not?" he said.

Celia laughed. "Her services *are* rather shorter, that is true. Knox is slightly terrifying."

"Who will win this battle, do you think? Knox or Queen Mary?"

"They are both strong-willed. I would not care to make a wager. And hopefully by the time matters come to a head between them we will be gone from here."

Lord Knowlton gave her a long, searching glance, studying her so closely she had to turn away. She had not spent all that much time in his company, but she had enjoyed his easy conversation. Being with him was simple—nothing like John.

Yet today Lord Knowlton's regard felt somehow different. He looked as if he wanted to discover something from her, about her. Everyone here said one thing and thought something very different. She had done the same thing for so long, always hiding, also cautious.

She was tired of it all.

She hurried her steps to catch up with the others, and Lord Knowlton stayed at her side.

"So you are eager to return to England?" he asked. "You do not care for Scotland?"

"Scotland is most interesting. I've enjoyed my time here," Celia answered carefully. "But, yes, I will be happy to return to England."

"And what will you do when you're there again?" Lord Knowlton said. "Will you remain in Queen Elizabeth's service? Or perhaps return to your family?"

What *would* she do in England? Celia had been trying not to think of that, to push away the future while she concentrated on her work here. Her brief time with John. But Knowlton's words made her realise how fast the future was bearing down on her.

"I have no family," she said. "So I will stay at Court for the time being."

"Perhaps you would prefer a household of your own?" he said quietly.

Celia looked at him, surprised by his words. "I would, but such things are not so easy to find, I fear."

He nodded. "I have been a widower for many years, Mistress Sutton, and it is a lonely life. But very soon I will have a great deal to offer a wife, if all goes as I hope."

"That is—very good. I am happy for you, Lord Knowlton," Celia murmured, not sure what to say. He had never spoken thus to her before, and she was bewildered.

Did he intend *her* for his wife? And what would happen to ensure his fortune? Did he also work for Elizabeth?

"Perhaps I may speak to you again on the subject when we return to London?" he said.

Celia simply nodded, and Lord Knowlton smiled at her as they kept walking. "Tell me, Mistress Sutton," he said. "What are your impressions of Queen Mary's Court? I am very curious…"

Celia was tired and puzzled as she made her way towards her chamber, weary of the effort of smiling and laughing with the Queen's ladies when all she wanted to do was find somewhere quiet to think. She had much to consider. The two Queens, Lord Knowlton, John—it was all too much.

At last she reached the door of her chamber and

pushed it open—only to find she was not to be alone after all. John lounged on her bed, leaning back lazily on the bolsters as he studied a stack of papers beside him. As she closed the door behind her, he looked up at her with a roguish grin.

Celia suddenly wished with all her might that he would *not* smile at her like that, would not confuse her even more, torment her with all she had once longed for and couldn't have. But truly he was not the one who did the tormenting. It was her own heart, her own feelings.

"I wondered when you would be returning," he said. "Do you feel properly pious now?"

"I feel it was quite unfair that you managed to stay here while the rest of us had to listen to the sermons of hellfire," Celia grumbled.

She put her gloves and prayer book down on the table and unpinned her veiled cap from her hair. As she smoothed the windblown strands she caught a glimpse of John in the looking glass. He'd braced his hands behind his head and leaned back as he watched her with hooded eyes. His doublet was open and his shirt clung to his chest and shoulders, reminding her of what he looked like naked. What they had done to each other last night in that very bed.

What she suddenly wanted to do again.

She licked her dry lips with the tip of her tongue and his stare sharpened. He sat up straight and watched her as she unfastened her surcoat and let it drop from her shoulders. She slowly untied the high frilled collar of the chemise that rose above the low, square bodice of her black velvet gown and parted the fabric.

"And did you learn anything enlightening today?" John asked, his eyes never wavering from her.

"Oh, a great deal." Celia tugged the pins from her hair and let the heavy dark mass fall over her shoulders as she took up her brush. "Lord Darnley is very good at counterfeiting piety when he wishes. And Knox practically froths at the mouth with hatred for women rulers. I fear Queen Mary would have done better to stay in France."

She drew the brush slowly through her hair, closing her eyes. She heard him leave the bed and move to stand behind her. The heat of his body wrapped all around her, drawing her closer to him.

He took the brush from her fingers and his hands slid slowly, caressingly, through the fall of her hair as he drew it back over her shoulders. She hardly dared breathe as she felt him ease the bristles through her hair.

"Anything else you observed?" he whispered in her ear.

"I think Lord Knowlton is going to propose to me," she blurted out.

The brush ceased moving and John tensed behind her, but only for an instant. Then the slow, gentle motions resumed. "Hardly surprising. Many men surely want to marry you, Celia."

But not you, she thought sadly. "He also said something rather odd about how soon he would be in a position to offer much to a wife."

"What do you think he meant by that?"

Celia shrugged. "That soon his fortune will increase, I suppose. They do say his present estate is rather modest. Perhaps Queen Elizabeth has promised to reward him, as she has with us. Or perhaps…" A thought suddenly struck her.

"Perhaps what?"

"It is silly. Lord Knowlton is the quietest, most mild-mannered gentleman I have ever met, and seems as devoted as any courtier to Queen Elizabeth. Yet Lord Burghley did say we would have to face French and Spanish spies who all have their own ideas of Queen Mary's marital plans."

She felt foolish even as she said it. Lord Knowlton? A foreign spy? But she had to think of such things. Suspect everyone.

Not that she could think much at all when John touched her like that.

"It sounds as if we should keep a closer eye on Lord Knowlton," John said. "And what will you say to his proposal?"

"He has to make one first," Celia murmured. "But I will have to marry someone, and he seems as good a choice as any. I doubt he is anything like my first husband."

"Should you not consider other offers first?"

She gave a bitter laugh. "Which offers would those be?"

He didn't answer. He dropped the brush and she felt him gather the length of her hair in his hands as he drew the slippery mass to his face and inhaled deeply. Celia let her head fall back until it rested on his shoulder, and he kissed her, open-mouthed and hungry, on her neck.

She reached up to thread her fingers through his hair, letting the short silken strands drift over her skin as he tasted her. His teeth nipped at her, and she gasped.

"Celia," he groaned, resting his forehead on her shoulder. "I've missed you so much, thought of you so much in all these years. Beautiful Celia…"

His words made her heart pound in her breast, as if it was coming alive within her after being frozen. Had he really thought of her as she had him? She felt such hope, but also fear. What did that mean for the past— and for the future?

She slowly turned in his arms and stepped back to look up at him. She laid her hands lightly on his shoulders and studied his eyes. He went very still under her touch, and his eyes were dark and full of stark pain. She had never seen him like that, and it made her tremble.

But she forced herself to keep watching him, staring into his eyes. Once she had hated him for making her love him and then leaving her. When she looked at him now she could see he was not the same impulsive, roguish young man who had swept away her foolish, girlish heart. He had seen things—things she could not fathom and which she longed to know. She wanted to know *him*, as he was now, every part of him.

She reached up and traced her fingertips over his face. She felt the sharply curved lines of his cheekbones and jaw, his knife-blade nose, the sweep of his brow. His eyes closed under her touch, and she drifted a caress over his lips. They parted and he caught her finger between his teeth and sucked it.

"John," Celia whispered. She went up on tiptoe and kissed his cheek. "John."

"I am here, Celia," he answered. He swept her up into his arms and carried her with him to the waiting bed.

She fell back onto the pillows and raised herself on her elbows to watch him. He looked back at her, his eyes hooded as he slid her shoes off her feet. His palms moved slowly up the back of her legs, pulling her skirts out of his way as he went.

He bent his head and kissed the sensitive spot behind her knee, his open mouth hot through her silk stocking. Celia let her head fall back and closed her eyes to let the feelings wash over her. She wanted to feel every touch, every kiss, every breath.

John loosened the ribbon garter and eased her stocking down and off before reaching for her other leg and doing the same there. As the white silk rolled down his mouth followed, a fiery trail over her skin. He licked over the arch of her foot and rose up between her legs to reach for the ties of her skirt.

Celia arched her hips to let him strip away her clothes. Every part of her he bared he kissed, slowly, reverently, as if he worshipped every curve of her body. It was achingly tender, and she wanted to cry from what it did to her. It was as if her heart was cracking all over again and letting him slip inside.

When she lay before him naked, he stood beside the bed to strip away his own clothes, his doublet and shirt tossed to the floor as his gaze never left her. She sat up and reached for the fastening of his breeches, unable to wait a moment longer to see him.

She peeled them away from his lean hips, down his thighs, until his erection sprang free. She caressed with her thumb that spot he loved until he pushed her away.

"Celia," he groaned.

Watching him, looking deeply into his eyes, she lay back down on the bed and opened her legs to him, welcoming him to come atop her and love her however he chose. Giving herself to him.

He seemed to see exactly what she was telling him. His nostrils flared and fire kindled deep in his eyes. She nodded, and he lowered his body slowly against hers, until she could wrap her legs around his hips and draw him to her. He slid along her, skin to skin, heartbeat to heartbeat, until his lips met hers in a soft, searching kiss.

Celia moaned at the touch of his mouth, at the way his tongue tasted the seam of her lips before sliding over hers, twining with hers. She *had* to touch him. She dug her fingers into his back, feeling the sweat-damp heat of his skin, the shifting and tensing of his muscles. They had come together so many times before, coupled as if compelled to each other, but in this moment she felt as if they were truly together.

One moment they were two people, two beings, then with a twist of his hips he slid inside her and they became one. He pressed forward until he was fully seated, his pubic bone pressed to hers, deeper than ever before. And then he rested against her, letting her feel their bodies together, feel him truly touching her.

"John, please…" she whispered, even though she

had no idea what she begged for. She just needed more, needed *him*.

And then he drew back, slow and steady, until he almost pulled out of her. When she cried out he thrust forward, harder, rougher, only to draw back again.

Celia grasped his taut backside and dug her fingers in tight, urging him forward, silently asking for him to make her his. To show her he was hers, if only for now. He braced his hands on the bed to either side of her and thrust hard. She heard his breath, heavy and intoxicating in her ear as he kissed her, and she couldn't breathe at all.

She closed her eyes and tilted her head back as she opened herself to him. She let him take her, hard and hungry, and felt her heart pound inside her breast as she reached for her climax.

"Wait for me, Celia," he growled. "Come with me."

"Yes," she panted. "Yes."

His movements grew faster, all rhythm gone to leave only hunger. Celia cried out as pleasure burst inside her, and he shouted her name as his back arched. She opened her eyes to see his features contorted with raw pleasure, the muscles in his arms taut.

And then he collapsed to the bed beside her, his hand on her hip. She had never felt anything like the peace that descended on her like a silvery cloud. She curled into his side, against his chest, and he pressed a kiss to her hair.

She couldn't say anything. She could hardly even

breathe. She could only slide into sleep again, held in John's arms. She never slept as deeply as when she was safe with him.

Chapter Nineteen

John smoothed his hand softly down Celia's bare back and over her scarred shoulder as he watched her sleep. Her skin felt so soft under his touch. Soft and slender—so vulnerable.

He slid his touch down her arm to take her hand, and thought how those delicate fingers held everything he was within their grasp.

She shifted against him, sighing in her dreams, and he lay down beside her again with his arm around her waist. Her hair drifted over his bare chest in a black cloud, and he buried his nose in the satin strands to inhale her perfume.

Their mission was drawing to a close and his time with Celia was slipping away. John closed his eyes on a spasm of pain deep in his heart. Something had moved inside him when he took Celia today. Nay—he had been changing ever since he saw her again that day at Whitehall. For so long she had lived in his mind as a memory, a dream, a beautiful and passionate young woman who had brightened his life for all too short a moment, given him hope for a different sort of life. He had seen so much that was violent, ugly and full of greed, and Celia was soft and as brilliant as the sun. Not sweet— never that—but even her tart tongue made him laugh. Made him live again, want to live again.

He had repaid all she'd given him with pain and trouble. Yet still he cherished every memory of their time together.

Celia now was so much more than he remembered. More beautiful, more brave. And when she'd lain back on the bed and held out her arms to him, surrendering to him, his soul had broken wide open and everything he was had flown free. She'd set him free.

And now he only wanted to keep her for ever, to make her his, even as he knew that could never be for them. Celia would never belong to anyone again—especially not him.

Not once he told her of his part in what had happened to her brother. He would have to tell her, he owed her no less now, and he would have to make amends for what he had done to all the people he had hurt in his service to the Queen. Part of his penance would be to lose Celia for ever, and then he would be only the hard, cynical shell he had always been without her.

But not yet. Not today. Today he still had her.

He slid down on the bed and moved the fall of her hair to kiss her shoulder. He wanted to heal those scars, to take away all the pain of her past. Her body undulated against him and she gasped as he kissed a hot, open-mouthed path down her back. He licked at the hollow just above the curve of her buttocks. His fingers caressed her softness there and she whispered his name.

"I am here," he answered. His fingertips brushed against the soft cheeks and she hissed.

John smiled against her skin and rolled her onto her back. He rested his chin on her stomach and looked up at her to find she stared at him with stormy grey eyes. Her pale cheeks were flushed with desire.

"Did I wake you, my fairy queen?" he said. "A thousand apologies."

"You aren't sorry at all," she answered. She slowly drew up her leg, brushing against his erection. He grew even harder at the merest touch of her skin. "Someone obviously seeks amusement."

"I watched you while you slept," he said, pressing soft kisses over her hip, her tight stomach, around her navel. "You looked so beautiful while you were dreaming."

Celia stretched her arms above her head, her whole body laid out for him. She closed her eyes and arched her back, sensual as a cat. "I was dreaming of you."

"Of me? And what exactly was I doing?" He bit at her hip, making her gasp again, and slid lower to kiss the inside of her thigh, just above her knee.

"Oh—something much like this, I think. Only a wee bit higher."

"Ah. Like here, mayhap?" He traced his tongue in a light pattern over the seam between her thigh and hip. Her legs fell further apart and he felt her fingers twine in his hair as she drew him closer.

"Or—here?" he whispered, and blew out a soft breath over her damp pink folds.

Celia moaned and her fingers clenched in his hair. "Aye, there!"

"You drive me mad, Celia," he groaned, tasting her sweet essence with the tip of his tongue. He needed her so much, felt so much. "The more I have of you the more I need you."

"I know, I know. Oh, John, I—"

Her words were broken off at the abrupt sound of a knock at the door. John reared up on his knees and automatically reached for the dagger under his pillow. Celia had gone perfectly still beneath him.

"John?" he heard Marcus call, as he knocked again. "I have to talk to you now. I know you are there."

John bit back a filthy curse and let go of the dagger. His friend had always had wretched timing. Even now his body ached and vibrated with lust, at the smell of Celia's arousal on his skin, her gasp in his ears.

But he also knew Marcus would not have come here if it was not vital. He would be off with Lady Allison or one of his many other women. John looked down at Celia, who stared back at him with wide eyes. She nodded and pushed herself up on the pillows, drawing the bedclothes over her nakedness.

John tore himself away from her and leaped from the bed. He scooped up his clothes, tossing her the shirt as he slid into his breeches. He drew the curtains around the bed before opening the door.

"What?" he growled.

Marcus's face was etched with concern, but as he

glanced over John's shoulder at the shrouded bed he grinned.

"I thought you might have been making a jest about seeking out Mistress Sutton," Marcus said. "Yet here you truly are."

John seized his friend by the shoulder and pulled him into the room. "What has happened?"

"And it had best be something very important, Lord Marcus," Celia called from the bed.

Marcus's grin widened. "Indeed it is. But I could be persuaded to delay my news if I did not know that my friend never shares."

John almost hit Marcus, but then he heard Celia laugh. She yanked the curtains aside, and he turned to see she knelt at the end of the bed. His shirt fell almost to her knees, covering her body even better than her satin gowns in folds of soft voluminous linen. Yet her black hair tumbled free down her back and her cheeks were pink, and he found he wanted no one else to see her like this. Ever.

Marcus was quite right. He did not share. Especially not Celia. He had no claim on her. Not really. But he wanted to. He wanted her to belong only to him.

He covered his emotions by tossing her the surcoat she had left on the floor. As she draped it over her shoulders he leaned against the bedpost and crossed his arms over his chest, glaring at Marcus.

"I don't care to share either," Celia said, far too calm for his taste. "And we are rather occupied at the moment. What has happened?"

"I was rather *occupied* myself," Marcus answered. "But I thought you should hear this."

"What is it?" John said.

"We have known all along that despite her strange infatuation with Darnley Queen Mary has been reluctant to make an English marriage. Now Allison has discovered someone is in the pay of Mary's Guise uncles and has been pouring out persuasions to accept *their* candidate instead—a certain Comte de Mornay. And Mornay has no love at all for the English. He would destroy any alliance, any chance of peace between the Queens."

"And there would be war with Scotland again," John muttered. "Even bloodier than under Marie of Guise."

"Who is this traitor?" Celia asked. "And how did Lady Allison find out?"

"She has become friendly with a certain Monsieur d'Alblay," Marcus said. "And that gentleman is not smart enough to guard his secret papers as he should. Allison is adept at reading codes. As for the Englishman taking French coin—it is Lord Knowlton."

"What?" Celia cried.

John swung towards her to see the flash of shock on her face, and he remembered that the man wanted to marry her. It made a spark of some dark emotion catch inside of him, thinking of her as another man's wife. "You are surprised about your suitor?"

"He did hint to me that he would soon be much wealthier," she whispered, as if to herself. "So he could take a wife."

Another spasm of anger passed through John's body. "And he wanted you."

"He admires you, Mistress Sutton?" Marcus said. He looked at Celia with a speculative glint in his eyes. "Perhaps he would talk to you frankly? Confess?"

"Nay!" John nearly shouted. "She will not be involved in this." She would not put herself in any more danger. He would not allow it. He would keep her safe.

Celia slid from the bed and came to his side. Her hand was soft on his arm. "I *am* involved, John. That is why I was sent here by Queen Elizabeth—to help protect her interests here. I confess I understand little of our true purpose here, and I have not done much to be assistance. It's obvious that Lady Allison is far more useful. But I *can* meet with Lord Knowlton. If I hint that his feelings are returned perhaps he will tell me more of the French plans."

"An excellent idea, Mistress Sutton," Marcus said. "It would make that part of our task much easier."

John nearly drove his fist into his friend's face. "Nay, it is no idea at all. You should stay away from Knowlton, Celia."

"He cannot hurt me here," she argued. "I won't let myself be entirely alone with him. I merely want to discover what he is doing in return for his newfound wealth."

"And we will stay near her, John," Marcus said. "No lady has ever been harmed in our care."

John stared down into Celia's grey eyes. She looked so calm, so cool and composed. Once she had been deeply hurt by him—more than once. He could not do that again. Not when he had vowed to keep her safe. Even from himself.

But her hand tightened on his arm. "I promised the Queen," she whispered. "And she will only help me if I help her. This task is small enough."

He remembered what the Queen had promised Celia in return for the task—a rich marriage, a secure future. All the things his own actions had stolen from her.

He glanced at Marcus, who watched them warily. If John did not agree to Celia doing this he knew she would just go with Marcus and do it anyway, without him knowing or being able to protect her. He looked back to Celia. She was cool-headed, calm. He knew she would keep her wits about her.

And talking, questioning—it was far less than he had done on missions in the past. He and Marcus would watch over her.

"No talking to him without us being near, even if it's in hiding," he said roughly. "And not until you are ready."

Celia nodded. "Of course."

"Excellent!" Marcus said with a grin. "Shall we meet tomorrow, then, on the ramparts? I will just leave you now to resume your—occupations."

He slid out of the door, and John and Celia were alone in the silence again. They merely stared at each other for a long moment and he tried to read her thoughts in her eyes. He could see nothing until the grey went smoky and a slow smile curved her lips.

She stepped back from him and let the surcoat fall from her shoulders. Never looking away from him, she reached for the hem of the shirt she wore and slid it over her head. She shook back her hair and stood before him naked, the light glowing on her skin, the rosy tips of her breasts pebbled.

All anger and worry fled as his stare avidly took her in, and all knowledge of the truth he would soon have to tell her. All he could see, all he knew, was her. Celia. Within reach of his arms. This had always been easy between them—perfect, fiery and full of delicious forgetfulness.

He reached out and wrapped his hands hard around her waist to drag her up against his body. He buried his face in the curve of her neck, smelling her, tasting her. His Celia. *His.* She would always be that, even when she hated him again. Even when she was gone from him.

"We still have the night ahead of us," she whispered, her fingers twisting in his hair. "However will we fill it?"

John growled in answer, and lifted her in his arms to carry her back to the bed. Her laughter echoed like the sweetest music in his ears.

Chapter Twenty

Celia slowly paced to the end of the lane, keeping close to the stone wall, and turned to walk back the other way. She hadn't expected to feel so nervous. After all, this was what she had come to Edinburgh to do—to deceive, discover. Yet her hands felt icy cold even in her gloves.

She drew her cloak hood closer over her head and tried not to glance at the doorway where John and Marcus, along with a young apprentice of Marcus's named Nathan, were meant to be hiding. The street was narrow and shadowed, quiet. So quiet she thought she could hear the snowflakes drifting to the ground. She felt so terribly alone.

She turned and walked slowly back to the end of the lane. She was meant to meet with Lord Knowlton under the apothecary's sign there, but what if he did not come? What if she failed before she even began?

Nay, she could not fail. She would have nowhere to go then.

"Mistress Sutton," she heard Lord Knowlton call.

She spun around to see that he had appeared at the end of the lane. He was also wrapped in a cloak against the cold, and for an instant there on the deserted, snow-dusted lane he looked ominous. Like a crow in a church-yard.

But he smiled as he reached her side and took her hand in his, even as his eyes flashed with a puzzled look. "I was surprised to receive your message," he said as he kissed her hand.

Celia shivered at his touch. Not with delight, as when John kissed her, but with something that felt strange, wrong. A surreal sort of haze seemed to come over her mind, as if she was not there at all.

"Not an unpleasant surprise, I hope?" she said. She managed to give him a smile.

He smiled back, but still that something flashed in his eyes. He tucked her hand in his arm and led her over to stand by the wall. "Not at all. You must know I've wanted to speak with you alone, without the distractions of the palace."

"Have you really, Lord Knowlton?"

"I had hoped my words to you when last we met were not too subtle," he said, still holding onto her hand, "and did not frighten you away. I have admired you greatly ever since we met."

"That is very kind of you. I have not been accustomed to admiration since my husband died."

"Do you miss being married as I do?"

Not at all. She had loathed being married, and something about that glint in Knowlton's eyes, the touch of his hand on hers, told her she would not enjoy it much with him either. But she had learned one thing in her marriage, and that was to conceal her true feelings at all cost.

She smiled and leaned into him, letting him feel her body against his. "Very much. It is lonely for a single woman in the world."

"Lonely for a man as well." His eyes heated as he looked down at her, took in her loose hair around her face, her parted lips. "I have had no one since my wife died."

"No one at all? A titled gentleman in the Queen's favour such as you?"

He shook his head, and raised one finger to trace the line of her jaw. She forced herself to stay still under his touch. "I have very specific tastes, Mistress Sutton. Celia. I want someone beautiful, sophisticated, but also a challenge. Someone not easy to conquer."

"Co-conquer?" Celia stuttered. She had not quite expected that from him. The kind, mild man she had enjoyed chatting with seemed to have vanished now that they were alone.

"You always seem so distant, Celia. So cool and composed." His palm traced down over the line of her throat, nudging her cloak out of the way so the leather of his glove was against her bare skin. "I have longed to know what you hide beneath all that disdain," he whispered. "To be the only one who can uncover your secrets."

Celia shook her head and fell back a step. His arm swept around her waist and brought her up against him. "I have no secrets."

"Oh, but I think you do. We all do."

"Do *you* have secrets, Lord Knowlton?"

"Of course I do. And they are why I can now take care of you as you deserve, lovely Celia. I can take you away from England to somewhere secret and safe, just the two of us, where we can share all our secrets."

Celia drew in a deep breath and forced herself to relax in his arms. Was this it, then? Was it really this easy to make someone confess?

"I will not live here in Scotland," she said.

He laughed. "Here, in this godforsaken place? Certainly not. Once my work is done we will live in a much more hospitable land. One where your beauty will be appreciated as it should be."

"Your work?" she said. Did she sound too eager?

His gaze narrowed on her and his arms tightened around her. "I cannot give away my secrets for free, my dear. I'll need something from you in return."

"I told you. I have no secrets to share. And I must be sure that whoever I marry will be able to care for me."

"You need have no doubts about *that* if we decide we suit." He lowered his head to press a soft kiss on her brow. "Show me that we will suit, Celia. That you are what I have been working for, waiting for."

"How?" she gasped as his parted lips trailed over her cheekbone. His kiss was hot, dry, seeking. It made her stomach seize in a painful knot.

"Kiss me," he demanded. He pulled her up on her toes and covered her mouth with his. His tongue forced her lips apart and pressed deep inside.

Celia screamed in her mind, over and over, as that

terrible trapped feeling she had always had with her husband closed over her. Black ice seemed to trickle over her body, freezing her, holding her fast so she could not move.

"You *are* a cold wench, aren't you?" he growled as his lips finally, blessedly, left hers. He nipped at her neck. "But we will soon change that."

Celia closed her eyes tightly and tried to pretend she was not really there. That she merely watched the scene from a distance, as at the playhouse. That was what she had done in her marriage. That distance was sometimes all that had kept her sane.

"I cannot marry a man who can't take care of me," she said again. "If you have Queen Elizabeth's favour…"

"Queen Elizabeth?" Lord Knowlton said bitterly. "She is nothing. England is nothing. The power in this world lies with France and Spain, and one day they will crush Elizabeth like the bastard upstart she is."

His harsh outburst shocked Celia after his earlier caution. She stared up at him, at his face that was so contorted she could hardly recognise it. "That—that is treason."

"It is merely the truth, as all wise men know." He suddenly tightened his arm around her waist and swung her hard to the wall, trapping her there with his body. "And if *you* are wise you will come with me before it is too late."

"To Spain?" she whispered.

"Spain?" He laughed. "There is no merriment in Spain. We will go to France, you and I, as soon as Queen Mary does what her Guise uncles wish. Despite

her foolish infatuation with Darnley she will soon remember where her true advantages lie."

At last the truth Celia sought. She closed her eyes
and tried to think. He had confessed, or as good as. It
would be enough for Elizabeth and Lord Burghley. Yet
he still had Celia trapped.

"You are allied with the French, then?" she said.
"They will give you the fortune that will let you marry
where you will?"

Immediately she knew she had pressed too far. His
body stiffened against hers. "Why do you want those
words, Celia?" he asked calmly. "I have already offered
you all you need."

Celia shook her head. "My husband lied to me. I cannot bear that again…"

"And did you lie to him?" His lips pressed hard to
the side of her neck, making her shudder. "Are you
lying to me now?"

"Nay!" she cried. Suddenly one of his gloved hands
was clapped over her mouth, strangling her words, her
breath. Holding her to the wall with his body, he reached
his other hand down to grasp the hem of her skirt and
drag it up over her leg.

Celia felt the cold wind on her skin, the hard trap of
his body on hers, and wanted to scream.

"Show me what a good wife you will be, Celia," he
said against her ear, and his hand swept over her thigh.

And then in an instant he was torn away from her.
Her breath flooded back into her lungs, painful and
cold, and she shook so hard she could scarcely stand.
She braced herself against the wall, and through the

filmy haze of tears she saw John throw Knowlton down into the street.

John had the man down on his stomach, his knee on Knowlton's back as he twisted his arm behind him. Celia had never seen John look like that before, his handsome face contorted with rage, with primitive fury. All his elegant sophistication was stripped away, leaving a killer in its place.

As she pressed herself back to the wall, watching in horror, John and Knowlton fought like dogs in the middle of the street, first one man and then the other down, until blood and sweat flew in the air. She almost screamed when Knowlton threw John to the ground, but John turned the tables yet again and had his opponent beaten down.

But when John staggered to his feet and started to turn away Knowlton suddenly snatched a hidden blade from inside his boot and lunged forward to drive it into John's side. John staggered back, staring down at the blood that had appeared on his torn doublet.

"John!" Celia cried.

He glanced at her for only an instant, then whirled around and drove his own blade into Knowlton's chest, twisting it until the man fell to the ground again, perfectly still, and the fight was over as quickly and violently as it had begun.

Celia ran to catch John's arm as he started slowly to fall, struggling to hold him up, to will her own life into him. To beg him silently not to leave her.

Suddenly Marcus was there. "Get John back to the palace," he said.

His firm touch on her arm seemed to be all that held her tethered to reality as she looked down at John's blood.

"Nathan will help you. I will take care of—that."

He nudged Knowlton's body with his boot, and Celia shivered.

"What if—? Did anyone see?" she whispered.

"If they did, they will know well enough to keep it to themselves," Marcus said roughly. "Go now. See to John."

Celia nodded. As the other man slid John's limp arm over his shoulder and drew him to his feet, she went to his other side and wrapped her hand over his waist. She could feel his breath dragging painfully in and out of his body, and she was glad for it because it meant he still lived. He was still with her.

"Celia, I am sorry…" he gasped.

She shook her head. "No talking, John. Save your strength now or we will never get you to the palace."

She glanced back over her shoulder as they carried John to the end of the lane, but Marcus, his assistant and Knowlton's body were already gone. The night was quiet again, as if the whole violent scene had never happened at all.

Except for the coppery tang of blood and steel in the air.

Celia shivered and turned away.

He couldn't reach her.

A thick, silvery mist swirled around him, concealing everything but the tantalising glimpse of Celia just ahead of him. Her black hair fell loose over her shoulders, and her smile was enticing as she called out to him. She held her hand to him, but when John reached for her she laughed and spun away.

"Celia!" he shouted, and the word echoed back at him, mocking him. A terrible desperation swept over him. He *had* to find her, grab her in his arms and know she was real. That she was his again and he could never lose her.

But she was gone. He ran through the mist, calling her name. He could hear her laughter, hear her whisper, "I am here, John. Right here," but he couldn't see her.

And then even her laughter was gone, and he knew with a horrible certainty that he had lost her. He was alone again, and he could never find his way free of that.

"John," she said again. "John!"

He spun towards the sound of her voice, hope rushing through him again. Foolish hope when he had thought he knew better than to allow such a thing. But there was no teasing laughter to her voice now, no enticement. Only fear and tears.

Nay, that could not be. Celia never cried.

John forced his gritty, heavy eyes to open and found himself staring up at a green canopy. There was no cold mist, only the warmth and smoke of a fire, the feeling of soft sheets against his bare skin.

And a cool hand on his arm, the summery smell of a woman's perfume. Celia's perfume.

He turned his head to see that she sat on the edge of the bed, staring down at him with her grey eyes. They were dark with concern, and they really did shimmer with the bright sheen of tears.

"Oh, praise God, you are awake," she said. "I feared you would open your wound with all that fierce thrashing about."

"Am I awake?" he said, and found his throat was dry. His body ached, the wound on his side was throbbing, but he would bear any pain if she would just stay there beside him.

"I hope so. You were feverish, but you feel cooler to the touch now." Her hand gently curled over his cheek and she smiled down at him. "Your eyes are clearer. I think you will recover."

John covered her hand with his, holding her with him. He turned his face and kissed her palm as he closed his eyes to inhale the sweet scent of her skin. "Because you were here with me. You brought me back."

"This has become a terrible habit of ours," Celia said. She raised her other hand to smooth back his hair, her touch light and gentle. "Nursing each other through wounds. You must take better care of yourself in the future."

John had to grin. "Why should I, when this is the result? You sitting at my bedside, not arguing with me, not flaying me with that sharp tongue of yours."

Celia pressed a fleeting kiss to his brow and drew away from him, leaving him without her touch. "That is not all I will flay you with if you do this again." She reached for a goblet on the table and held it to his lips. "Drink this."

John took her wrist between his fingers. "Not poisoned, is it?"

Celia snorted. "I wouldn't have worked so hard to heal you only to do away with you now. It is merely healing herbs in wine. Queen Mary herself sent her finest stock of French wine for you."

"Queen Mary?" John drank deeply, draining the goblet before he lay back on the pillows. The wine seemed to restore him so she could think clearly again.

"Aye. She is quite distraught that an emissary of her 'dear cousin' would be treated thus in her own city." Celia laid aside the goblet and moved to sit on a stool by the bed. John saw she wore one of her black gowns, but it was rumpled, as if she had sat there in it for a long while. Black tendrils escaped from the braided knot of her hair. "She has sent home Lord Knowlton's French contact and written to Queen Elizabeth with her apologies."

"How long have I been here, then?" he asked.

"Only two days—three as it is nearly nightfall now. Queen Mary moves quickly when she wishes to." A small smile touched Celia's lips. "She also cries a great deal."

"And has she made up her mind to marry?"

Celia shrugged. "I doubt a French alliance of any sort now. She says only that she finds Queen Elizabeth's advice to marry an Englishman very sound. And she was dancing with Lord Darnley again last night."

"You saw them?"

"Nay, I was here, nursing a hot-headed rogue through

a nightmare. Lady Allison told me. She is much sharper of wit than I would have guessed."

John winced. "It is what makes a good intelligencer. The ability to hide one's true self, to be whatever one needs to be at the moment."

"And you are a good intelligencer, are you not, John?" she said quietly.

He looked at her. Her tears were gone, her cool, pale mask back in place. It made him want to grab her and hold her hard, until his Celia came back from behind that mask. "Until I lose my head and find myself wounded, aye," he said.

Celia nodded. "How did you come to this work?"

John's eyes narrowed as he studied her face, her hands folded in her lap. What did she know? What did he dare tell her now? And yet he could not hide from her any longer. He cared about her far too much, owed her too much.

A wave of weariness washed over him, and he closed his eyes and let his head fall back. What was in those cursed herbs? He couldn't tell her everything right now—not when he didn't have the strength to make her understand, make her forgive him for his long-ago betrayal.

"I was a wild young man—aimless, angry. I wanted only to fight, craved violence, but there were no wars to fight then, where I could utilise my energy. It came out in tavern brawls, brothels, trouble of all sorts."

Celia nodded. "You were sent to the country?"

"After a spell in Bridewell, after a friend of mine killed a man in a brawl I was involved in, my uncle de-

cided I needed a quiet place to contemplate my sins."
That was true. He didn't add that Lord Burghley had
given him the chance to redeem himself by breaking a
conspiracy against the Queen, and that his reward for
succeeding had been more and heavier tasks. Matters
that had kept him away from her for too long, things
he'd had to protect her from.

"But there I just committed more sins," he said bitterly.

"Was I your sin?" Celia asked. "But I wanted what
happened—wanted you. I have never felt like that before, from the first moment I saw you."

"Nor had I. You were—are—unlike anyone I have
ever known. I knew then that I should stop, that I should
stay away from you, but I could not." He still could not.
Something about her kept drawing him back to her,
over and over again.

"I am glad you did not," Celia said quietly, firmly.
"What happened between us sustained me through everything that happened after."

John's heart gave a spasm of pain, a raw ache at the
hurt he had caused her. That he had caused himself
when he'd had to leave her. "Celia…" he said tightly,
knowing he had to tell her everything. Had to make it
right somehow.

But the chamber door opened and the hand John
had started to hold out to Celia fell back to the bed.
Lady Allison stood there, her shrewd gaze sweeping
between them. She set the tray she held down on the
table and smiled.

"I have brought you some supper, Sir John, and come

to relieve you of nursing duty for a time, Celia," Allison said. "You must be very tired."

Celia nodded wearily. "Thank you, Lady Allison. I *am* tired." She rose from her chair, watching John as he stared back at her. He would read nothing in her eyes now. "I will be back in a few hours."

John stared after her until the door closed behind her. He could still smell her perfume in the air. He heard the rustle of Allison's silk skirts as she settled herself in the chair, and turned to see her knowing smile.

"Well," she said, "who would have thought such a simple-seeming task could cause such trouble? You look wretched, John."

"What a charming flatterer you are, Allison," he said, closing his eyes. "A veritable silvery-sweet tongue."

She laughed. "Your friend Marcus seems to like it well enough. But, alas, the two of you will be going back to England soon, while I must stay here and mind Queen Mary. So dull for me."

John's eyes opened. "Going back to England?"

"Aye, Queen Elizabeth's orders arrived by messenger today. You are urgently needed in London—though I think you must travel at a rather slower pace at the moment."

"And Celia?"

Allison shrugged. "You will have to ask her, I think." She drew a small book from the pouch tied at her waist and settled back to read. "You should rest now. I fear there is still much more work to come."

Chapter Twenty-One

❦

"Will you be happy to go home?" Lady Allison asked Celia as they strolled through the Queen's private garden at Holyrood.

"Home?" Celia said. She wrapped her cloak closer against the cold day and watched Queen Mary and her ladies as they gambolled with their little dogs amid the trees. She had no home to go back to; she could hardly remember what a home felt like at all. A place that was hers, where she belonged. She had been a prisoner or a guest for too long.

Only when she was in John's bed, wrapped in his arms, did she feel she was meant to be there. And it felt too good, too frightening.

She realised Allison was looking at her quizzically. She had been silent for too long. She smiled and said, "I will be happy to see England again."

Allison laughed. "You don't care for Scotland?"

"It is a strange place. A rough one." Celia studied the craggy face of King Arthur's Seat rising beyond the palace. She remembered John's crumbling family home. "But beautiful in its own way. I'm glad to have seen it."

"But also glad to leave it behind, I think?"

"Perhaps." Scotland had been a dream, Celia thought, a moment out of her real life when she had found John again, had come alive again when she had thought herself dead inside. How could she regret that, even if the dream-time had to end? She could not be sorry.

Yet she felt so fragile inside, as if she was barely held together. One cold wind would shatter everything.

"I'm not sure what waits for me back in England," Celia said. "But I must face it soon. I cannot stop time."

"Perhaps you could do more services like this for Queen Elizabeth," Allison said quietly. "It has its own rewards."

Celia looked at her, still unused to seeing such a solemn look on Allison's pretty face. She couldn't fathom how she'd missed it before, how she had failed to peer behind the façade.

It made her frown, wondering what else she had missed.

"Have you been doing such work for a long time, Lady Allison?" she asked.

Allison shrugged, and the hood of her cloak shifted from her red hair. "I was the daughter of an earl who was sadly impecunious. When I was fourteen he married me off to a much older man."

In those simple words—the tale of so many young ladies—Celia could hear a vast amount of pain. Had she not experienced that herself? "Were you married very long?"

Allison shrugged. "A few years. I learned many useful things from my husband. He was—demanding in the bedchamber, even though he could not often become aroused. When he died I found myself without money again."

"So you worked for the Queen?"

"Aye. Lord Burghley saw what I could do and gave me a task to prove myself. Then another and another. I do well for myself, and serve England as well."

Celia stopped at the end of the pathway, listening to Queen Mary's laughter, the shrill barking of the dogs. She could only think of John, of all her old foolish hopes. Hopes she had dared to resurrect even as she knew better.

"Do you never want anything else?" Celia asked.

"Such as what?" Allison said with a small smile. "I have no wish to marry again. Especially to another man who is not my own choice. I am content."

And Celia envied her that. To have work she was good at, a purpose. To serve something important, larger than herself, and be free to do it. It was what John did.

"I was wrong about Lord Knowlton," Celia said. "I never suspected him. How can I do what you do when I can't read people?"

"You learn that," Allison said. "Once you know a few things people can be shockingly transparent. Most people." She laughed. "I could never understand *you*, Mistress Sutton."

Celia had to laugh in return. "I cannot understand myself at times. But how did you learn to do this?"

Allison's face softened. "Marcus helped me when we first met. He and John have been doing this work longer than I have."

"And do you often work together?" Celia asked, pushing away a small pang of jealousy. It seemed it was Marcus Allison had the soft spot for, not John. Even so…

"With Marcus, aye. Not so often with John. But we were all in Paris together for a time, working to discover a traitor in the embassy there. There are always those ready to take French coin, just as Knowlton was. It was a dangerous time."

"But you all survived?" Celia whispered, afraid that might not always be the case. Her hands were suddenly cold, her brain numb at the thought.

"Aye, we watched each other's backs. John had just finished with the Drayton conspiracy when he was sent to Paris, and I don't know what happened to him but he was fiercely looking for a fight. Even the French could not stand against him."

Celia froze. Arthur Drayton was the name of her brother's friend—the one who had embroiled him in his traitorous scheme. Surely she had heard Allison wrong? Surely—? Nay, it could not be. It could not! She wouldn't let it be. And yet she feared it *was* the truth— the truth that had always been staring her in the face even as she denied it.

Clutching at her cloak with numb hands, she spun towards Allison. "What did he do before he went to Paris?" she whispered.

Allison frowned, as if she was disquieted by what

she saw in Celia's face. "Lord Burghley knew there was some sort of trouble brewing, and that John's uncle lived nearby. He was sent to ferret out the traitors there. Once he did that he was sent immediately to France. You have turned very pale, Mistress Sutton. Are you ill?"

Celia shook her head. She felt as if she had been turned into a block of ice. Her face, her skin, her heart were so cold, and thoughts raced through her head.

Of *course* John had not really been sent to the country to atone for some scandal. He had come to trap her poor, foolish brother and his friends in their silly game of conspiracy. William had never had a chance against a cool, deceitful predator like John Brandon. And neither had she.

She had fallen into his bed like a ripe plum. But at least then she had been a naive girl who could not know better, who had never encountered anyone like him before. Now she was a woman, a widow, who knew she should guard her heart. But she had gone to him again, opened herself to him again.

She was a doubly damned fool. And she could feel her heart cracking inside her and falling into a thousand shards of doubt.

"I must go inside now," she said tightly.

"I will go with you," Allison said, but Celia shook her head.

"You stay with the Queen," Celia managed to say. "I am well. I only need to rest for a while."

And to kill John Brandon. But even if he was gone from her life, gone from the world, she would never be able to banish the hollow pain inside of her. The pain had been diminished for a time, while she lay in John's arms, but now it was back, a steel vice on her soul.

She had the terrible certainty it would never be gone again.

She turned and walked away. She forced herself to move slowly, to make her steps measured even as she wanted to run. She still walked slowly when she reached the palace, climbed the stairs past the courtiers who swept past her laughing and stood whispering in niches. They were all a blur to her.

Her mind felt quiet, hazy, as if time had ceased to have all meaning. She felt nothing at all. The pain had gone too deep. If only she could go on feeling thus the rest of her life.

As she turned onto the quiet corridor lined with closed chamber doors she reached up to unfasten her cloak. She didn't notice as it dropped to her feet. Her eyes were on the door to John's chamber, the innocent-looking wood that concealed the mouth to hell.

She pushed it open without knocking and stood frozen on the threshold. John was packing books and papers in a valise, wearing a loose shirt over his bandage, his hair tousled. He looked so beautiful, so much like the John she had loved, that her heart gave a painful squeeze within her.

But that John had never existed except in her own foolish mind, Celia reminded herself. *This* John was a hardened intelligencer, a liar. He had destroyed her brother, her family, her whole life.

Yet she loved him still, and that only made her hate him more.

He glanced up, and a smile spread across his face at the sight of her. His eyes lit up a brighter blue than any summer sky.

"Celia," he said. "What do you do today?"

The sound of her name on his lips made the ice that encased her crack violently. Flames of utter fury roared through her—fury at him for making everything between them a lie, at herself for wanting to believe him. She lunged towards him and caught his cheek with her nails. The long scratch on his golden skin stoked her anger higher, and she slapped him with the flat of her palm.

Caught by surprise, he fell back a step and she slapped him again. With a scream, she tried to strike once more, but he was ready for her. Her fury gave her an abnormal strength, yet he was still much stronger. He caught her wrist, his fingers like steel manacles, and swept her arm behind her back as he spun her round, her back to his chest. His other arm banded around her waist.

"How could you?" she cried, and to her horror felt hot tears spill down her cheeks. She kicked back at him, twisting against his arms, but her skirts tangled around her legs and bound her in place. "I hate you."

"Hush," John growled against her ear. He easily evaded her strikes, holding her bound against him. "Hush now, Celia."

"You killed him," she sobbed. "And I let you. I let you deceive me because of my foolish lust for you, and he died because of it."

John's body went rigid against hers. "You know."

A tiny, foolish part of her had actually hoped he would deny it. That part died at those quiet words, and Celia went limp in his arms. The angry fire burned away, leaving her cold again. So cold.

She slumped in John's arms and let her tears fall. They had been held back for so long. "So it is true. You were sent to find the traitors, break their conspiracy."

"Aye," he said roughly. She felt him lower his head and press his face to her hair. His breath was harsh against her. "That was why I went there. It seemed a simple enough task. But I never expected you, what you would do to me."

Celia closed her eyes and sniffed back the last of her tears. She turned her damp cheek into his shoulder, but the familiar smell of him made her heart twist again. "Did you use me for information? Suspect me?"

He gave a bitter laugh. "If you remember, Celia, we seldom had time to talk at all. You never told me anything. They gave themselves away easily enough."

"But then why…?"

"Why did I take you? Because I *had* to. I knew it was wrong, foolish, but I had to have you. No woman has ever made me feel as you do, Celia, so wild, insane with need for you. My fairy queen." His tone was rough, strained, as if he held back a flood of emotion.

Celia gave a ragged sob. Her whole body felt weak, empty. "Do not call me that."

"I am sorry, Celia." He was silent for a long moment, their breath the only sound in the room. "Have you done with beating me now?"

"For the moment," she said. She felt too weak and sad

even to lift her arms. There was nothing but the numbness. Remorse that she had let herself trust in him again against everything. She was a fool, a fool.

John carefully lifted her in his arms and laid her on her back on the bed. She closed her eyes and turned her head away, achingly aware that he stood over her, watching her intently. At last she heard him walk away and sit down on the stool where she had sat for so many hours while he was wounded.

"I was going to tell you," he said.

"When?"

"Soon. Or perhaps long years from now, when you were too old and weak to attack me like that. But I did know that after everything we had been through you deserved the truth."

Celia still could not open her eyes, could not look at him. "Why did you not say before…?" Before she'd made love with him again. Opened her heart to him again.

She heard the rasp of his hand rubbing over his bristled jaw. "Because I was weak and selfish. I wanted this time with you. Needed it."

"There are dozens of other women who would happily warm your bed. Why toy with me again?"

"God's blood, Celia, but it is not like that with us and you know it," he cursed. "I know it was wrong of me, but I had to have you again and I would have done anything to get you."

Celia wanted to cry again, to sob out all her hurt and confusion, but she simply had no tears left. She had nothing left at all.

She slowly pushed herself up until she sat at the edge of the bed. John didn't move, but he watched her as closely as a hawk watched a mouse, as if he could read her and know what she would do next.

But he couldn't know. She didn't even know herself. She wanted to demand he tell her why he had done this to her again, what it was about her that set her up for hurt like this. But she did not want to give him the satisfaction of knowing what she felt.

"Well, then, you had me, John," she said. "And I had you. But no more. Never again. I have nothing more to give anyone."

"Celia, I beg you—" he began, but she held up her hand to stop him.

"I need to be alone now," she said. "Please don't follow me."

She slid off the bed and moved towards the door on trembling legs. John moved to help her, but at the touch of his hand she flinched away and took a step back.

"Celia, this is not over," he insisted.

"Not now," she whispered. "Please, not now. If you care even one tiny bit for me, John, you will let me go now. I might shatter if you touch me." She could not connect with him again. She did not trust herself any longer.

She felt the tension in his body, the urge he had to grab her in his arms again, yet he made no move towards her. Celia wrapped her arms around herself tightly and moved to the door. She felt cold and fragile, and very, very old.

Once the door had closed behind her she ran. She

scooped up her cloak and kept running until she was alone in her chamber. She collapsed to the floor, her hands over her face, and wished the terrible ache would go away. That she could just be numb again for ever.

But she feared the hurt would never, ever be gone.

John smashed his fist down onto the table, scattering papers everywhere. Pain drove up his arm but he didn't even notice it. All he could see was Celia's face as she turned away from him. So pale and still, with eyes that were void of any light. Dead.

And *he* was the one who had done that to her. To Celia, the woman he loved.

"I love her," he whispered, and the truth of those words was like a bolt of burning lightning, illuminating what had been hidden in darkness for him for too long. What he had hidden from himself.

He loved Celia, and he had lost her. Because of his own actions, his past, he had hurt her far worse than her hell-damned husband ever had.

"God's teeth!" John shouted, and swept the table clean with a vicious swipe of his arm.

He had to go to her, make things right for her again. He would give her anything, *be* anything, if she would just trust him again as she had when she took his body over hers.

Full of violent desperation, John swung towards the door and flung it open, intent on finding Celia. But Marcus stood on the threshold, blocking the doorway. His friend's face, usually so full of humour and mischief, was solemn. He shoved John back into the room and slid inside, slamming the door behind them. He crossed his arms over his chest and blocked the exit.

"Whatever this is, Marcus, I have no time for it now," John growled. "Get out of my way."

Marcus shook his head. "So you can go to Celia Sutton?"

John froze, his hands curled into tight fists. "Aye."

"What is between the two of you?" Marcus demanded. "I thought she was merely some kind of challenge to you, an unattainable lady for you to try and seduce. But now your quarrels are the talk of the palace."

"She was never *merely* anything to me," John admitted.

"Then what? Why are you running after her now, with that violent look in your eyes? I have seen that look before, right at the moment you ride into a tournament."

Violent? Aye, he did feel violent. As if he could grab Celia and hold her fast between his body and the wall and force her to listen. To understand, to forgive. Even if he knew her forgiveness was impossible now. He would do anything to get her back, but that would only drive her further away.

John slumped down onto the stool and ran his hands through his hair. "I knew her before…years ago."

Marcus relaxed his stance, but still stood by the door. "And you had a youthful affair that ended badly? One you renewed here in Scotland?"

"Aye, something of the sort," John muttered. "Do you remember the Drayton conspiracy?"

"Of course. You more than proved your worth on that one."

"Her brother was one of the men involved, but I did not know he was until after I had made love to Celia. He was executed and her family ruined."

"Curse it," Marcus breathed. "And she did not know before?"

"Not until today. I was going to tell her, but she found out somewhere else. Now she despises me."

"Then that is why…"

"Why what?"

"Allison told me Queen Mary has arranged an escort back to London for Mistress Sutton and they are to leave at dawn tomorrow."

"She is going already?" John burst out. "Then I must see her now!"

"Nay, John, that would not be a good idea! She needs time to think," Marcus protested.

John shoved him out of the way and tore open the door. He ran hard through the corridors, seeking her chamber. Her door was locked, but he could hear the murmur of soft voices inside.

"Celia!" he shouted as he pounded his fist on the door. He drew startled glances from passing courtiers, but he did not care. All he knew was that she was leaving, and time grew so very short.

"Celia, I know you are in there," he said, resting his forehead on the door. "Please, just listen to me for a moment."

There was a long silence, then the sound of a bar being drawn back. The door opened a small amount and Celia peered out at him. Her hair was drawn back tightly again, and she wore solemn, unrelieved black.

Her eyes still held that flat, stone-grey deadness.

"John, please," she said softly, tonelessly, "there is no more to say."

There was everything in the world to say, John thought as he stared down at her. She was right before him, and yet she was as unreadable as if oceans were between them. All he could say, all he could feel, was, "I am sorry."

"Sorry for what? You were doing your task. I merely got in your way." She sounded so bitter as she looked away from him, her whole body stiff and still. "It will not happen again."

"Because you are going back to England without me?"

"Queen Mary has agreed to provide an escort. Queen Elizabeth will want an account of what happened here. You will not have me to burden you any longer."

"Burden me?" John could not hold himself back any longer. He caught her hand in his, holding it fast. Her skin was cold and she did not draw away. But neither did she yield, and he had to restrain that primitive urge to push her down, hold her until she gave in and admitted what they were to each other.

"Celia, tell me how to set this right," he demanded. "Tell me how to prove to you I have changed!"

She shook her head. "You do not have to prove anything to me, John. Please, I am tired. Let me go."

"Nay, Celia. Not until you let me tell you all that happened."

"I know what happened! It doesn't matter now. Nothing matters." She wrenched herself free and slammed the door.

John pounded his forehead on the wood that lay between them and rested his clenched fists against it to keep from pounding the barrier down and claiming Celia as his own. It wouldn't work now, he knew that well—not when that coldness was upon her. He had to cool his temper, wait and plan.

Celia *would* be his again. There was no way either of them could be without the other now. She simply did not know it yet.

Chapter Twenty-Two

Celia stared down into the rushing water of the river far below where she stood on the edge of the bluff. The water was a cool grey-blue, dotted with lacy chunks of ice, and she remembered all too well how it had felt when she'd fallen in and it had closed around her. How it had felt when John pulled her out of the cold depths and saved her life.

She closed her eyes and shivered. But it wasn't the bite of the wind. It was the memories that made her feel so cold on this journey home. It had been days since she'd left John and started to make the long trip back to England, and she had thought she could leave him behind. Forget him and how she had given her heart to him—again.

But the images bombarded her at night in her dreams, and during the long, cold days. Images of John's face as he made love to her, his stark intensity as they moved together. His smile as they danced, his fierce protectiveness as he shielded her from the blast. So many memories, overlaying those of that past, so much deeper and richer than the wild moments of their youth.

So much more hurtful now, when she felt as if she had glimpsed John's true soul and let him see hers.

Celia turned away from the river and walked along the bank as she listened to the echo of her escorts' conversation as they rested for the midday meal. She hadn't been able to eat or be still since they'd left Edinburgh. She kept turning John's words over in her mind as she tried so hard to make sense of the past and the future. To make sense of him and how he made her feel.

As she walked now, the sound of the rushing river in her ears, she made herself remember her brother. William had been older than her but had always seemed younger, in the way he'd been so easily seized with strange passions and ideas. He had been her parents' darling, their heir, their hope for fading fortunes, but even they had seemed to realise he could be as changeable as mercury.

When the Queen's men had come to their house and arrested him for his part in his friends' conspiracy, Celia had been shocked and grieved, but there had been little surprise. It had seemed the sort of wild fancy he would have. But it had cost him his life and her parents the last of their fortune. And it had been John who had found William out. The man she had begun to love with all the fire of her young heart.

The man she had begun to love again with all her wounded soul.

Celia shook her head hard, as if she could rid herself of her troubled thoughts and emotions, but they clung stubbornly. The fury she'd felt when she had first found out about the true nature of John's work had burned itself out in the cold, solitary days since. Her rational knowledge of how the world really worked had begun to come back again. Her brother had gone against the Queen's law in his foolishness and would have inevitably been caught. John had had no choice in what he'd done.

But he *had* left her. That she could not understand. She needed to hear it from his own lips, needed to know if she had meant anything to him. And she had things she had to tell him as well.

It was time to lay the past to rest and move into the future.

Celia turned and strode back to camp, sure now of what she had to do.

Chapter Twenty-Three

She was back where it had all begun, as if nothing had happened at all.

Celia looked around the crowded presence chamber at Whitehall and remembered when she'd stood there all those weeks ago, watched those same people waiting, whispering, desperate for Queen Elizabeth's attention. It looked the same, sounded the same, and yet it was not the same at all. Things *had* happened, and she had changed profoundly.

But she was still alone.

She rubbed at her arms through her purple satin sleeves as if she was chilled, even though the close-packed bodies and the roaring fire created a humid heat against the freezing rain outside. She stayed in her shadowed corner and ignored the curious stares around her. She could hardly see them anyway.

She just saw John, the last time she'd glimpsed his face before she had closed the door on him. That final glimpse had haunted her on the long journey back to

England—that image of anger and passion and something she couldn't even recognise on his handsome features. His voice demanding she listen to him.

A swift glimpse of his family's house on her journey—the place where they had stayed together, held each other, talked—had almost torn out what little was left of her heart. She had glimpsed John's past there, what had driven him to do what he did now. She had seen what might have been a home.

But she could not have listened to him after that—not when she was so raw, so furious. She wasn't sure if she could ever listen. He had betrayed her not once but twice, and she in her infatuation had let him.

The journey had given her time to be quiet and think, to start to mend her heart again, but she was still so very confused. She needed to talk to him, to make sense of everything that swirled in her mind and heart.

Celia studied the crowded chamber, the swirl of fine velvets and silks, the taut voices and brittle laughter. She saw in her mind all that happened—John, Queen Mary and Lord Darnley, Holyrood, Marcus and Allison—had it been real? Or had it been a dream, and this room the only reality?

"Mistress Sutton?" she heard someone say behind her, and she snapped out of her daydream to turn and see one of the Queen's pages.

"Yes?" she said.

"Her Grace will see you now."

Celia followed the man through the crowd and past the guards at the doorway. Just as at that first meeting, she was taken through a series of chambers into the inner sanctum of the Queen's own room, where the page bowed and departed and Celia was left alone with Elizabeth.

They were truly alone now. There were no ladies on the scattered cushions and stools, no Lord Burghley hovering. The household was soon to move to another palace, and there were open crates and cases around the room. The Queen sat at the table by the window, a quill in her long fingers and papers scattered before her. She wore stark black and white today, her red-gold hair pinned atop her head with pearl combs.

Elizabeth glanced up and smiled. "Ah, Mistress Sutton. You have returned to us."

Celia sank into a curtsy. "I have, Your Grace."

"Are you happy to be back in England?"

Happy? Celia wasn't sure she understood that word now, not for a long time. "Very much."

Elizabeth gestured to her, jewelled rings sparkling in the firelight. "Then come, sit here with me, and tell me about Scotland. You trapped a villain, so I understand."

"I played a very small role in that indeed," Celia answered as she lowered herself onto a stool across from the Queen.

It was John who had fought Lord Knowlton, John who had been wounded, who'd killed the man. John who had done so many things to change her life.

"That is not what I have heard." Elizabeth sat back in her chair and tilted her head as she studied Celia thoughtfully. Her careful solemnity in that moment was a contrast to her cousin's merry laughter. "You helped rid us of a traitor in the pay of the French. We owe you our thanks."

Celia swallowed. "Yet I fear I failed you in your request."

"Concerning my dearest cousin's marital intentions?" Elizabeth said. She tapped her fingers on the table. "Aye, I did hear she is quite infatuated with Lord Darnley. She is nursing him through a bout of the measles even as we speak. But you did not fail me, Mistress Sutton. You helped me a great deal."

Confused, Celia shook her head. "But Your Grace…"

"Do you think me foolish, Mistress Sutton?"

"Not at all, Your Grace!"

Elizabeth laughed. "Good. Growing up, I had to learn to read people very closely, to learn their real fears and desires. To know what they were going to do even before they did it. It was the only way to stay alive at times. I sense you have lived in much the same way, Mistress Sutton."

Celia could only nod. Her entire life had felt that way until John.

"Aye. You also know that sometimes we must make our hearts cold, deny what we want in order to do our duty. My cousin has been a queen since she was born. She does not understand these things. She doesn't know what it feels like to lose everything. I knew she would never marry Lord Leicester, or I would never have offered him to her."

"Oh," Celia breathed. A slow understanding dawned in her mind, a realisation of how clever Queen Elizabeth had been. How she had moved them all in her game—even Lord Burghley and Darnley.

"You see, Mistress Sutton? I couldn't allow Mary to ally herself with France or Spain again. It is too perilous. Nor could I give her my Robin. She would not have appreciated him. And he would be too strong a consort. Darnley, on the other hand…"

"Is a cruel, drunken knave," Celia whispered.

"But a handsome one, charming when he wants to be, and from a family almost as close to the throne as Mary's. He could maintain a façade long enough to draw in a woman desperate to be married again. Once the crown matrimonial is on his golden head…"

"Disasters will likely ensue," Celia said. "Very clever, Your Grace."

"Thank you, Mistress Sutton. But you spent much time at my cousin's Court. Do you think my little scheme will work?"

Celia thought of Mary's hand on Darnley's arm, the way she'd laughed with him as they danced. The loneliness in her eyes that Celia understood too well. "Very probably. Queen Mary seems ripe for romance."

"Then you did serve me well." Elizabeth rose from her chair and went to the window. She pushed it open to let in the cold breeze, staring out at the garden below, and Celia saw a quick spasm of pain pass over her pale face before her queenly mask fell into place again.

"I can't help but envy my cousin in one respect, Mistress Sutton," she said softly.

Celia laughed. "Having Darnley as a husband?" She could not imagine such a thing.

Elizabeth laughed too, and gestured for Celia to join her at the window. "Nay, never that. I would never choose so poorly. Only that she *can* choose—that she can be married and have someone beside her. A throne can be a cold place alone—as can life."

Celia peered past the Queen's shoulder to the garden. A man walked there, tall and broad-shouldered in a green velvet doublet, his black hair covered by a plumed cap. Lord Leicester. He also looked alone as he strode down the path. Elizabeth watched him, her fingers clutching the window frame.

"You have been married, Mistress Sutton," she said. "Do you miss it?"

"Nay, Your Grace," Celia answered honestly. She did not miss being married to Thomas Sutton at all.

"Yet you would accept a marriage as a reward for your service to me?"

Celia shrugged, wishing she could push away that old longing for a home, a place to belong. "I have no home, Your Grace. I need a place to be."

"Yet we don't need marriage for that." Elizabeth slanted a speculative look at Celia. "How did you fare on the journey with John Brandon?"

The sound of John's name, so unexpected and sudden, seemed to hit Celia in her soul. She didn't know what to say, and stared down at the garden. "Sir John?"

"He is handsome, is he not? Half my ladies are in love with him. Yet he won't let any of them near—not really. When you two met here..." Elizabeth shook her head. "I *see* people, Mistress Sutton, as I told you. I know things they don't even know themselves. But you may leave now. I will consider your reward."

"Thank you, Your Grace." Celia bobbed an unsteady curtsy and made her way out of the chamber.

Such a strange conversation. She scarcely knew what to make of it. Did the Queen know what had happened with her and John? How could she, when Celia hardly knew what had really happened herself?

She walked slowly up the stairs, nodding at greetings, feeling numb and removed from the scene around her. She didn't know where she was going until she found herself at the door of her chamber.

She pushed it open and stepped over the threshold— only to find John sitting on the edge of her bed.

He watched her as she slowly closed the door behind her, not smiling, his blue eyes glowing.

"Good day, Celia," he said. "I trust you had a fruitful meeting with the Queen."

Chapter Twenty-Four

"So you have returned to England," she said slowly. Her eyes greedily took him in—every detail, every inch of him. She had thought of him every day on the long journey home, had gone over every word they had shared, all the touches and kisses. Now he was here, with her again, she didn't know what to say.

She wanted to run to him, throw her arms around him and feel that he was really there with her again.

Yet he was not *with* her. The short distance between the bed and the door might as well be the distance between Edinburgh and London.

"I left soon after you did and rode hard the whole distance," he said.

She could see the marks of a fast journey on his face, the harsh lines and dark circles under his eyes that spoke of weariness. His hair looked damp, as if he had just washed it, pushed back from his face to reveal the austere, elegant lines of his features. His doublet was a fine Court garment of crimson velvet, but was only half fastened.

"Such haste," she murmured.

"I had to see you again," he said.

His own stare roved hungrily over her face, as if he had missed seeing her. Had he truly missed her? Thought of her when they were apart?

The thought, the longing, made something raw crack inside Celia again. She wrapped her arms around herself tightly as if she could hold it in. Could contain all the emotions that threatened to burst free when she thought of all that had happened in Scotland.

"I wanted to run after you—to run your horse to ground and pull you into my arms until you listened to me," he continued harshly, staring into her eyes. "To *make* you understand."

Celia couldn't bear the look in his eyes, so hungry and hard, for another moment. She shifted away. "Why did you not?" she asked as she went to peer out of the window. She couldn't even see the half-frozen river below through the haze in her eyes.

"I wanted to. Every primitive instinct in me told me to!" he said ruefully. "But Marcus held me back. He said you needed time to be calm, to think about all that had happened, and that I needed to think as well. He was right."

Celia gave a choked laugh. "For miles after Edinburgh I half wanted, half feared to hear you coming after me."

"What would you have done if I had?"

"I do not know. Hit you. Screamed at you. So Marcus was quite right to urge caution."

She heard a soft rustle as he rose from the bed, the

fall of his booted steps on the floor as he crossed the room to stand behind her. He was so close she could feel the heat of his body wrap around her, his breath on the nape of her neck. She trembled and closed her eyes.

"Do you want to scream at me now, Celia?" he said quietly. "Do you hate me?"

She thought she felt the light touch of his finger on her hair, but when she let her head fall back it was gone. Nay, she did not hate him. Perhaps for one moment, in that searing hurt when she had found out what he had done, she'd hated him. Now she knew what kind of world he lived in, what he had to do to survive. Now her feelings were so much more complex, so tangled.

"Did you use me back then, John? To find out information about what my brother and his friends were planning?" she demanded. That question had haunted her for days. "Was that all I was to you? Tell me the truth."

"Never, Celia," he said firmly.

His hands closed on her shoulders and spun her round to face him. His eyes burned with a pale blue fire, and she feared she would fall into them and be consumed. Lost.

"I knew you had nothing to do with your brother's actions. I only..."

"Only *what*? Tell me! I need to know."

John shook his head. "I tried to stay away from you, but I could not. Every time I tried you would draw me back to you with just a kiss, a smile. I had never felt anything like it before. It was like an irresistible force."

"An irresistible force," Celia whispered. "Aye, it was

the same for me. I *needed* you. You were all I could see."
And she feared she still needed him. Would always need
him despite everything.

"I never wanted to hurt you," he said softly.

"My brother's actions were foolish and he paid for
them," she said. "You could not have stopped him. Nor
could you have betrayed the Queen because of him. I do
see that now." Because of her own actions in Scotland
she saw the world so much more clearly.

"Before I went to Paris I came back to find you," he
said hoarsely, his hands tight on her shoulders. "I knew
I should not, but I couldn't stay away. I wanted to beg
you to come with me."

Celia gasped, and shook her head as if she would
deny his words, the hurt and hope of them. "But you
did not! I never saw you again until that moment here
at Whitehall."

"It was your wedding day." There was a world of
pain in his voice she had never heard from John before.
It made her want to cry, to weep at what was once lost.
What she still wanted despite everything.

"I saw you from a distance on your way to the
church, in a blue gown with flowers in your hair," he
said. "I did not know the truth of Thomas Sutton then.
If I had I would have snatched you from the road, forced
you to go away with me no matter the consequences.
But then I thought you were better off without me."

"Better off without you?" Celia cried. She pressed
her hand to her mouth to hold back the ragged sobs. "I
missed you so desperately for three years, John! Ached

with the loss of you, the fear of what had happened to you."

"I ached for *you*, Celia. Thought of you every day. But I imagined you safe with your family, a home of your own. Content with your life after the terrible things I had done. If I had known—God's blood, Celia." He pulled her against him, one hand cradling her head to his shoulder as he held her fast. "Can you ever forgive me for all I have done?"

Celia pressed her face into the soft linen of his shirt and breathed in deeply. Tears ached behind her eyes, but she couldn't let them free. Not yet. "Do you love me, John?"

"I love you so deeply, Celia, so fiercely that I know I can never be free of it. I am yours."

With that she cried, letting the tears fall down her face even as she laughed. Her heart, so closely locked and guarded for so long, cracked open and hope and joy flew into the world. She was free.

She tilted back her head to smile up at him, and he framed her face in his hands as he hungrily took in every part of her. Tears and exultation both. Everything she was.

"As I am yours, John. I love you," she said. "I will forgive you everything, for ever, if you will only promise never to leave me again."

"I could never leave you, Celia," he said. "You are trapped with me for ever now, come what may."

For ever. Celia had never heard sweeter words. She went up on her toes as John's lips claimed hers, hard, hungry, and in that kiss she tasted what the words love and for ever truly meant. The past was gone, the pain banished, and all they had now was each other.

He was hers and she was his. For ever.

Epilogue

Scotland, One Year Later

"Lady Brandon! Whatever are you doing up there?"

Celia turned around at the maidservant's shriek, the corner of the tapestry she was holding up clutched in her hand. The table she stood on was hard and smooth under her stockinged feet, and felt perfectly solid. "I'm trying to see what this would look like here, of course, Mairie. It has just arrived from London, and I think this wall is the place for it."

"Then you should have called for me, or for one of the pages. Sir John would be so angry if he saw you standing up there in your condition."

"I'm being very careful, I promise," Celia said calmly. She laid her hand over the small bump under her satin skirt, as yet still almost undetectable. But in a few months there would be the music of a baby's cries in these corridors and chambers that were finally coming to life again after all these years.

Celia let Mairie help her down from the table to the flagstone floor, and as she smoothed her skirts she studied the hall around her. It was very different from when she had first seen it, the night John had brought her there to shelter her from the storm and told her of his family's history.

When Queen Elizabeth had sent John back to Scotland after their marriage, as part of her delegation to Queen Mary's Court, Celia had despaired of making it a real home. Now the rooms were cleaned and refurbished, filled with fine furniture and colourful tapestries, and painted cloths, new glass in the windows, and warm rugs on the floors to keep the Scottish chill away. But the very best thing to keep the cold away was surely the hours she spent with her husband in the cocooned, sensual privacy of their curtained bed. There John kept her warm every night with his caresses, his wondrous kisses, the words of his love she had lived without for so long.

"Here, my lady, let me hang the tapestry for you," Mairie said. "You should sit by the fire for a while. You mustn't get too tired."

"I'm not tired at all," Celia said, blushing at her thoughts. But she let Mairie take the heavy cloth from her.

As she watched the maid clamber up onto the table there was a sudden commotion in the entrance hall, the boom of voices and the clatter of spurs.

"Sir John is home!" Celia cried. She spun round and dashed out of the room, her skirts clutched in her hands, even as Mairie called after her with a warning not to run. John had been to Edinburgh for many days, and Celia had begun to think he would never return.

But now he stood there in their home again, the cold wind sweeping around him from the open doors, his hair tousled and his black velvet and leather clothes creased from the hard ride home. He looked weary from his journey, but a brilliant smile touched his lips when he saw her and he opened his arms. Celia ran into them, holding onto him as if he was the most precious treasure in all the world.

"My fairy queen," he said roughly, lifting her from her feet as he buried his face in her hair. "How I have missed you."

"As I've missed you," Celia said. "Welcome home, husband."

And as he kissed her she knew they had truly both found their home, their hearts' deepest desire, at long last. Together.

* * * * *

Author's Note

When I wrote my book *The Winter Queen*—the story of Anton Gustavson and Rosamund Ramsay—I was very intrigued by Anton's cousin Celia Sutton. She seemed so unhappy, so haunted, and I wanted to know why! I wanted to know what had happened to her, and what it would take to make her believe in love again.

I so enjoyed spending time with her and her gorgeous hero in this story. I also enjoyed researching the story's setting and learning more about Mary Queen of Scots. I knew quite a bit about her late life in English captivity, but not much about her early days back in Scotland after years in France. It was fascinating to read about this time in her very complex and tragic life, but very hard not to shout warnings at her not to marry Darnley!

Her life does indeed slide into disaster after her marriage, just as Queen Elizabeth predicts. For a detailed look at the events surrounding her marriage and its violent unraveling I like Alison Weir's *Mary Queen of Scots and the Murder of Lord Darnley*.

Celia and John's part in the tale is fiction, of course, but much of what happens to them and the people they meet is part of history. Mary and Darnley, Elizabeth and Burghley—and their disagreements over Mary's marriage—Mary's four Marys, the terrible weather on Darnley's journey to Scotland, Mary's efforts to recreate a French Court in the rougher environs of Scotland, her religious feud with John Knox, even her excursions out into the city dressed in men's clothes, are all things I enjoyed incorporating into the story. It also seemed like the perfect backdrop for Celia and John's tumultuous romance!

If you'd like to read more about this period, there are many, many sources on Mary Queen of Scots. Here are just a few I enjoyed:

—John Guy, *The True Life of Mary Stewart, Queen of Scotland* (2004)

—GW Bernard, ed., *Power and Politics in Tudor England* (2000)

—J. Keith Cheetham, *On the Trail of Mary Queen of Scots* (1999)

—Roderick Graham, *The Life of Mary Queen of Scots: An Accidental Tragedy* (2009)

—Antonia Fraser, *Mary Queen of Scots* (1969)

—G. Donaldson, *All the Queen's Men: Power and Politics in Mary Stewart's Scotland* (1983)

—M. Swain, *The Needlework of Mary Queen of Scots* (1986)

—Jane Dunn, *Elizabeth and Mary: Cousins, Rivals, Queens* (2003)

—Caroline Bingham, *Darnley: A Life of Henry Stuart, Lord Darnley, Consort of Mary Queen of Scots* (1995)

—James Mackay, *In My End is My Beginning: A Life of Mary Queen of Scots* (1999)

—Alison Plowden, *Elizabeth Tudor and Mary Stewart: Two Queens in One Isle* (1984)

—S. Haynes, ed. *State Papers of William Cecil, Lord Burghley*

—JS Richardson, *The Abbey and Palace of Holyroodhouse* (1978)

Plus the guidebook to Holyrood, now available at the palace—the photos were invaluable!

COMING NEXT MONTH from Harlequin® Historical

AVAILABLE OCTOBER 16, 2012

SNOWBOUND WEDDING WISHES
Louise Allen, Lucy Ashford, Joanna Fulford

This Christmas, as the snow begins to fall, wedding dreams are made against a beautiful Regency backdrop. Enjoy three wonderful tales you'll never forget.

(Regency)

UNCLAIMED BRIDE
Lauri Robinson

After stepping off the stage in Wyoming, mail-order bride Constance Jennings waits for her husband-to-be, who never shows up. Single father Ellis Clayton must be the only man in town *not* looking for a bride. But his young daughter's habit of rescuing wounded critters means he ends up offering Constance a temporary shelter. One that he quickly wishes to make more permanent!

(Western)

HOW TO SIN SUCCESSFULLY
Rakes Beyond Redemption
Bronwyn Scott

With his comrade rakes-in-arms succumbing to respectability, wicked Riordan Barrett might be assumed to be next. Until Riordan finds himself not only an earl...but father to two young wards! This rake needs help—and hiring sweet, innocent Maura Caulfield as governess won't be such a hardship. He'll show her just how much fun sinning can be....

(1830s)

RETURN OF THE BORDER WARRIOR
The Brunson Clan
Blythe Gifford

Once part of a powerful border clan, John has not set eyes on the Brunson stone tower in years. With failure *never* an option, he must persuade his family to honor the king's call for peace. To succeed, John knows winning over the intriguing beauty Cate Gilnock holds the key....

(Tudor)

REQUEST YOUR FREE BOOKS!

 HARLEQUIN® HISTORICAL:
Where love is timeless

2 FREE NOVELS PLUS 2 **FREE GIFTS!**

YES! Please send me 2 FREE Harlequin® Historical novels and my 2 FREE gifts (gifts are worth about $10). After receiving them, if I don't wish to receive any more books, I can return the shipping statement marked "cancel." If I don't cancel, I will receive 6 brand-new novels every month and be billed just $5.19 per book in the U.S. or $5.74 per book in Canada. That's a savings of at least 17% off the cover price! It's quite a bargain! Shipping and handling is just 50¢ per book in the U.S. and 75¢ per book in Canada.* I understand that accepting the 2 free books and gifts places me under no obligation to buy anything. I can always return a shipment and cancel at any time. Even if I never buy another book, the two free books and gifts are mine to keep forever.

246/349 HDN FEQQ

Name _____ (PLEASE PRINT) _____

Address _____ Apt. # _____

City _____ State/Prov. _____ Zip/Postal Code _____

Signature (if under 18, a parent or guardian must sign)

Mail to the **Reader Service:**
IN U.S.A.: P.O. Box 1867, Buffalo, NY 14240-1867
IN CANADA: P.O. Box 609, Fort Erie, Ontario L2A 5X3

Not valid for current subscribers to Harlequin Historical books.

**Want to try two free books from another line?
Call 1-800-873-8635 or visit www.ReaderService.com.**

* Terms and prices subject to change without notice. Prices do not include applicable taxes. Sales tax applicable in N.Y. Canadian residents will be charged applicable taxes. Offer not valid in Quebec. This offer is limited to one order per household. All orders subject to credit approval. Credit or debit balances in a customer's account(s) may be offset by any other outstanding balance owed by or to the customer. Please allow 4 to 6 weeks for delivery. Offer available while quantities last.

Your Privacy—The Reader Service is committed to protecting your privacy. Our Privacy Policy is available online at www.ReaderService.com or upon request from the Reader Service.

We make a portion of our mailing list available to reputable third parties that offer products we believe may interest you. If you prefer that we not exchange your name with third parties, or if you wish to clarify or modify your communication preferences, please visit us at www.ReaderService.com/consumerschoice or write to us at Reader Service Preference Service, P.O. Box 9062, Buffalo, NY 14269. Include your complete name and address.

HHI1B

RUNNING FROM THE PAST...
SHE BUMPS INTO HER FUTURE!

Read on for a sneak peek of Lauri Robinson's fresh and exciting debut novel from Harlequin® Historical.

UNCLAIMED BRIDE

Not only was she out of her element, her wardrobe was as out of place in Wyoming as the ocean would be. What she wouldn't give for the red velvet cape lined with rabbit fur she'd left England with. She'd sold it, along with a few other of her more elegant pieces, hoping to find a way to financially support herself. The amount she'd gained had paid her room and board for the week, but hadn't been enough to replace the overcoat, let alone anything else. That had contributed to her ultimate decision—become a mail-order bride.

The way Ellis Clayton glared down his nose at her made Constance doubly wish she'd never seen Ashton's first letter.

When his gaze met hers, he asked, "Are you interested in coming home with Angel?"

Constance forced herself to breathe. The men across the road still leered, but other than the wind, it was deathly quiet. Besides herself, Angel was the only trace of a female she'd seen.

Knowing the man waited for an answer, Constance prayed the thickness in her throat would allow words to come out. "Perhaps, I…" Her mind couldn't fathom a single suggestion. Fighting to hold an iota of dignity, she voiced her options, "I apologize, but at this moment, your generosity appears to be my only hope."

The man's expression softened and the sight did

something to Constance's insides. She couldn't figure out exactly what, but then again she'd been greatly out of sorts since stepping off the stage.

His gaze went to his daughter, who smiled brightly. After shaking his head, he gestured to one of the men. "Put her stuff in my wagon, would you, Jeb?"

Angel grabbed Constance's hand, and tugged her in the man's wake. "He's not as grumpy as he makes out to be."

The girl's assurance didn't do much for the quaking in Constance's limbs, nor the churning in her stomach. She willed her feet not to stumble as she matched Angel's quick pace into the building. Nonetheless, Constance sighed at the relief of being out of the wind.

Will mail-order bride Constance Jennings
be able to make a home and find love in
Cottonwood, Wyoming?

Find out in
UNCLAIMED BRIDE
by Lauri Robinson
Available October 16 from Harlequin® Historical

HHEXP1112